the big dink

SMASH POINT SOCIAL
BOOK 1

CYNTHIA GUNDERSON

with gratitude

Editing and Critique
Jordan Truex, Scott Gunderson

Cover Design
Ink and Veil

Assistants and Sanity Support
Kyra Schroeder, Desri Wulandari

one

WATCHING Garrett Davis talk on the phone is more entertaining than TikTok. Since his office is directly across from mine, I'm privy to a show at least once per hour, and the guessing game to determine what phone call he's on still hasn't gotten old. Especially since I let slip the existence of said game to Sam—my coworker, best friend, and sole reason I wake up every morning to brave the hellscape that is Denver traffic—the other night at the pub.

"Wait. You have a rubric? For judging his phone conversations?" Her eyes narrow like a hawk that's locked in on a mouse scurrying through a corn field. After two years of daily interaction, she knows me better than my own parents.

"I mean, it's not that official."

"You said 'grading sheet,' Alecia. That sounds fairly official."

Ok, so that part is true. I had a coupon for a free customizable paper product from All Star Print, the company we use for all of our mailers. Our company didn't have a use for it, so after briefly considering a bulk order of

Tinder business cards for Sam, I figured I'd make my little hobby more convenient.

"It's just a notepad." Skepticism writes itself all over her face, and I know what she's thinking. Since my last breakup, Sam has had me on a strict regimen of rewiring my brain. I'm excellent at understanding what other people want. Also quite adept at molding myself into that woman at the expense of my actual beliefs and opinions.

But that isn't what I'm doing here. I'm not changing anything for him. It's good to learn more about the man you're interested in. This was simply a matter of curiosity and thoughtfulness.

"A normal notepad?" Sam asks.

I tuck my hair behind my ears. The pub always gets loud past eight, and I can barely hear myself think. "It's a little bit custom."

Sam laughs with a shake of her head, her chestnut curls bouncing. Somehow, even after a full day at the office, she looks like she just got a blowout. "That is . . ."

"Unhinged? Yes. I'm aware."

"No. I was going to say exactly like you. To make a game in the first place, but then to arbitrate with rules—"

"I'm not arbitrating. It's just a way to keep track."

"Of what?"

We're in it at this point. There's no use trying to hide anything. I scroll to the recent files on my phone until I find the template I submitted for printing, then I turn the screen toward her. "So the first section details body language *before* the phone is ever answered."

Sam purses her lips, attempting sobriety. "Okay."

"Sometimes he leans back in his chair before he answers. I think he's trying to do that whole, 'Things are going perfectly. Why wouldn't you want to choose us as your partner?' thing that he always pulls out at vendor fairs."

Sam nods. We recently witnessed his showboating at FanX. "So it's someone from work."

"I'm getting to that. That's in the next section. There have to be multiple check boxes from the same category for it to be a slam dunk."

Sam sips on her margarita as I move on to the next section. The options there are: perfect posture in his chair, hunched over his desk, jumping up to stand, or chair swiveled around with his back to the glass.

"Oh, what's that one?" Sam points to the chair swivel.

"I've only seen him do it three times. I'm still trying to figure it out. Sometimes hunched over the desk can be combined with laughter or heavy sighs—"

"Never his sales voice?" Sam moves her finger up the screen.

"Never his sales voice. Sales voice only comes into play when the chair is leaned back or he's standing. So, if I have 'leaning back in the chair' plus 'sales voice,' I'm seventy-five percent sure it's a work call, but there have been a few times when category three tipped the scales."

Sam reads through the options. "Hand touches face, hand runs through hair, fingers pressed to bridge of nose."

"It's the hands through his hair. I swear there's something different about those calls."

"What do you think it is?"

I lean in, but don't lower my voice, since a handful of babies, likely CU Denver students, are belting out the chorus to a Sabrina Carpenter song. "The other day, his door was open. Mine was cracked."

Sam nods. "As always."

"Right. And I overheard pieces of the conversation. They

sounded work-related. He was talking about a contract with Hills and Co—"

"Oh, yeah. We finished that deal last Friday."

"Exactly, but here's the thing." I pause for dramatic effect. "He was giving compliments."

Sam's head jerks back like I flicked her nose. "Compliments?"

"Mmhmm. Things like, 'You did an excellent job with that,' and 'Well, of course, it worked. It was your design.'"

Sam's hand flies up to clutch her theoretical pearls. "He did not."

I hold out my hands as if to say, "case closed." The evidence is irrefutable.

"Garrett's sleeping with someone at the office."

My smile borders on maniacal. "No. Not sleeping with someone. *Wants* to be sleeping with someone. Remember when he was with Molly or—"

"Mel."

"Yeah. Whatever. Those phone conversations? Never happened. He and Mel only ever texted." What I would have given for a screenshot of those messages, based on his facial expressions alone.

"Well, maybe that was because of Mel."

I raise an eyebrow. I can't blame Sam for being so oblivious. She wasn't the one with the approaching-unhealthy obsession with our coworker. "What does Garrett always do before he nails a contract?"

"Constant contact. Usually a gift or two. Lots of—Ohhh." Sam realizes it before she finishes her sentence.

"Right. Phone calls. And then as soon as he has it in the bag?"

"Text and emails only."

"Exactly."

"So you think there's someone he's interested in. But he hasn't sealed the deal."

I nod, leaning back in my chair and folding my arms. The student has become the master.

"Well, we have to figure out who it is."

My thoughts exactly. I shouldn't have waited this long to bring Sam in on my guilty pleasure. She's been all in on every crazy adventure even before we started working together. The Bubble 5k, thrift store marathons, Pokémon GO missions. This was child's play. "I'll bring you a notepad tomorrow."

Sam looks genuinely concerned. "You have *more of them?* How many did you print?"

I didn't answer that, but I kept my promise. Now, Sam and I both have a phone call tracker sheet hiding under knickknacks on our desks. It's all incredibly convenient, as Sam, in her corner office, has a perfect view of the breakroom.

Just the other day, she noticed him answer a call while waiting for a new pot of coffee to brew. There was bridge-of-the-nose pinching combined with heavy sighs. With the lowered voice, we concluded it had to be family. Not what we were looking for, but still good information. By my calculations, he'd had four more family calls than usual in the past week and a half.

Why, you might ask, do I feel so motivated to keep such dedicated surveillance? That's simple. I've been in love with Garrett Davis since Sam got me the interview here at Paper and Pixel eight months ago.

Garrett is traditionally handsome. Tall and lean with shoulders and arms that announce his gym membership, a head of thick, dark hair that he always wears product in, and baby-blue eyes I want to dive into and swim a few laps in. He wears LuLulemon slacks and collared shirts with the sleeves always rolled up, featuring micro prints on the insides of the cuffs.

On top of that, he's whip-smart. As one of the founders, he helped build the company while he was in high school, from nothing but an inkjet printer and a contract with his mom's real estate agent. He knows how to land the whales. He is brilliant at it, sitting across from CEOs twice his age, dissecting clauses with a million-dollar smile, flipping objections into signatures. Every time he emails over a fresh contract, signed and sealed, it feels like watching a magician pull money out of thin air. And maybe that's why I can't help myself. Because how do you not fall for the man who can talk anyone, even a Fortune 500 shark, into saying yes?

There's no way I'll use any of my reconnaissance against him, but having information about him has already proven useful. After the day with two family calls in a row, I happened to bring in Parlor Doughnuts for breakfast. That earned me eye contact and a "What's your favorite flavor?" which I'm still second-guessing my answer to. Maple was so cliché. Completely forgettable. I should've gone with matcha or lemon basil. Because as Garrett always says, "We don't sell products, we sell the story they tell." And I sold basic vanilla.

My phone buzzes on the desk. A message from Sam.

911

My mouth goes dry. Sam doesn't use emergency codes for low toner. This either means I've royally screwed over a client or . . . possibly hobby notepad-related? Either option is equally panic-inducing.

I push my chair back so fast it spins, and bolt out the door into the hall, jumping back when I nearly collide with—

Mother of pearl. Garrett.

"Where's the fire?" he asks. With eye contact. And a crooked grin. My stomach is suddenly swimming with live eels.

"Oh, uh—just excited to talk with Sam about the Corren project."

He raises an eyebrow, and his whole face shifts, turning into something new. That's the thing about Garrett. I swear he must've been the one popular theater kid in high school. His entire being is a study in character. "That's exciting to you?"

I smooth my hair, scoffing. "Not like *exciting*, exciting, if you know what I mean." *What the hell was I saying? To a guy I worked with?* "I mean, I'm just—" *Don't say excited, any other word but excited.* "Arous—" NOT THAT ONE! "Motivated to build that relationship. I think it will open the door to other opportunities in the tech space."

Sweat trickles between my boobs. I pray my neck isn't breaking out in hives, but my skin is already starting to itch. I give it three minutes before I need calamine.

He taps his Apple pencil against his forefinger. "Nice. I agree." Garrett gives me one last look, then strides into his office.

I agree? He made a joke, smiled at me, *and* agreed? This was quickly becoming a day for the history books.

I rush down the hall and slide into Sam's office, but

before I can word vomit the past five minutes, I process the expression on her face. "What happened?"

She winces. "I'm so sorry, A."

"What?" I stumble to the chair in front of her desk, my mind spiraling through worst-case possibilities. Did I forget an order? Send a personal email to a client? That happened once before, and I'm already reliving the shame of telling a reporter from 9 News that I was expecting my period on Tuesday.

Sam motions to a chair in front of her desk. "You should sit down."

"Sam, I swear—"

"I'm serious."

I drop into the upholstered swivel egg, holding her gaze like we are in a staring contest to the death.

When I think I might spontaneously combust, Sam finally blows out a breath. "I know who it is."

two

I BLINK, Sam's words sitting on the surface before finally sinking in. "Wait. You mean—?"

She nods, biting her lip. "Garrett met her in the breakroom. They talked. He ran his hand through his hair—"

I gasp, my hand flying to cover my mouth. Each of those three data points is shocking in its own right. Garrett doesn't loiter in the breakroom, nor does he meet people and chat.

Sam's smile is apologetic. "He offered to carry a signboard that looked like it weighed less than my left sandal to the admin desk. For her."

Who was this vixen? This fictional woman who could inspire such out-of-pocket behavior? "What the hell, Sam? Say the damn name!"

"You're not going to like it."

"Well, I don't especially enjoy sitting in purgatory, either!"

"It's Megan." She says the name like she'd recently read it on an obituary.

My body goes rogue. First, my stomach plummets like

an elevator cable snapped. Then my throat clenches shut as if I'd eaten a pound of shellfish for lunch.

Megan is one of our top designers. If I didn't already have a crush on Garrett, she would be next on my list. Not only can she put together creatives that turn me into a seagull spotting something shiny, but she is the closest thing to a Sidney Sweeney look-alike I've ever seen.

Soft, dirty blond hair that hits the middle of her back. Perfect hourglass figure. Doe eyes and high cheekbones.

"Girl." Sam stands and rounds the desk, holding out her arms. She has to press my head into her ample bosom because I can't force myself to move.

"I can't compete with all that." I mumble into her sweater.

"Well, her personality—" Sam starts, but I pull away.

"Her personality is more addictive than Reese's Christmas Trees, are you kidding? She's always smiling, she never panics with deadlines, she says kind things about everyone, even that guy in design with the handlebar moustache—"

"Geez, you make it so difficult to help you feel better." Sam's face is still pinched into a grimace.

My body turns gelatinous, spreading over the chair like a suicidal starfish. "Her voice is like the silky narration from those sleep stories on YouTube."

"I think some of them might actually be her . . ."

"Serious?"

Sam nods. "I heard Nina talking about it. I guess she used to do some modeling and commercial work."

Of course she did. It absolutely tracks that Megan would excel at everything. That she chose this job because she loved it, not because she didn't have better options.

I close my eyes, draw in a deep breath, and attempt to

keep my chin from wobbling as all my dreamy romantic subplots with Garrett crash and burn. It's not that I need it to work out with him, but I'm twenty-four and my dating history has been patchy at best. I spent the last two years complaining about how men are the problem, but the proof is right in front of me. He's putting effort in somewhere. Just not with me.

"You never know . . ." Sam drops my arms and walks back to her desk, rifling in her drawer for our emergency chocolate.

"You never know, what?" I groan.

Sam returns, forcing a square of Argentinian 75% dark into my mouth. "Maybe it'll just be a fling."

"A fling?" I suck on the chocolate for a moment, then give in and chomp.

"Yeah. Like you said, Garrett is a closer. He likes to sign the contract, then move on to the next thing."

I did say that. She has a point. "But what if she's the one who changes that? Keeps him interested forever?" Of anyone, Megan is capable of that. She's like the sweet, innocent daughter of a business mogul in small-town romance novels. They always win over the CEOs, convincing them to leave their high-profile jobs to bake bread in a small shop in the mountains.

Sam shrugs, dropping to half-sit on the edge of her desk. "What if she's not?"

I wet my lips. Okay. Not impossible. I can work with that.

My executive functioning comes back online with the influx of theobromine now in my system. "What was the board?"

"Hm?"

"You said he carried a board."

Sam blinks. "Oh, yeah. I have no idea. I saw the fingers in the hair thing and—*Alecia!*"

I'm already halfway out the door. Sam follows me down the hall, bumping into my back as I pull to a halt at the admin desk.

"Hey, Nina." I flash my most winning smile. It's nothing like Megan's.

She flicks her eyes up from her monitor. "Morning."

I scan the desk, the wall, the— "Oh, wow! Is this new?"

The poster board sits propped against the wall on the thin strip of side counter we just passed. *Paper and Pixel Pickleball Club* is written in gorgeous, loopy calligraphy across the top. Handwritten, not printed. Damn it, Megan is a goddess.

I force my eyes down to read the details. Fridays after work at the new club, The Court Collective, that opened a few blocks down on Eighteenth. Then I see the sign-up on the clipboard next to the pin-up. Garrett's name is at the bottom of the list.

Hope bubbles in my chest. This whole thing might not be about Megan. Garrett loves pickleball. Ever since The Court Collective opened, he's been bringing his bag to work. The first time I saw him emerging from the men's restroom wearing a white T-shirt and shorts that hit him mid-thigh, I almost fainted.

But did Megan play? Why else would she plan something like this if she didn't? Unless it was a team-building exercise she'd volunteered for. That was absolutely something she would do.

I scan the list and find her name at the tippy top. The first person on the list. This was her idea.

Daaaang. She's into him, too. She has to be. Even if she volunteered to organize an extracurricular, there are a thousand different options. But this one equates to sweat, tank tops, and tiny tennis skirts.

I do the mental math. First day of the club is—I check the calendar on my phone—October 10. That gives me—

"Red flag, A," Sam hisses.

I scoff. "What? This is a recreational activity. I do actually like sports." True. I probably wouldn't have ever considered this one had Garrett not signed his name on the line, but relationships were supposed to broaden your horizons, weren't they?

"It's barely a week and a half."

I reach for a pen from the cup organizer on the countertop below. "I played tennis in high school."

"Pickleball isn't tennis! I don't think?"

The truth is, neither of us has any idea, but how hard could it be? There's a net and a racquet or paddle—something to smack the ball with. Easy, peasy.

I hand the pen to Sam, fluttering my eyelashes. "I hear learning a new sport is really great for mental health."

"You know what's not great for mental health? Rediscovering your lack of athleticism in front of all of your coworkers."

I press my palms together. "We'll take lessons together." The plan is already taking shape in my mind. Plenty of time. We'd have at least a couple of lessons and time to practice in between. All I have to do is find an instructor and open courts. Not at The Court Collective, obviously. We don't want anyone here getting wind of our extra practice.

"I'm not a sports person," Sam insists.

"How do you know, huh?" I nudge her, guiding her hand to the sign-up.

Sam hesitates a moment, then locks her eyes on mine,

and I know I'm in for it. "You know that Oktoberfest bar hop?"

"The one on the pedal cart? Sam—"

She brandishes the pen like a weapon. "You're doing it."

I grit my teeth, my eyes flicking between the ballpoint and the sign-up sheet. This could be my last chance to make an impression before Megan unintentionally convinces Garrett to give up the company and buy a bakery in Granby. I could endure six hours trying to figure out how all of the pedals on that cart were connected to make the wheels move in one consistent direction. "Fine. I'm in."

Sam nods with approval, then scrawls her name under mine. "Find us some damn lessons."

three

IT TAKES ME A FEW DAYS, but I finally find a
place for lessons, and Sam and I dutifully show up at our
time on Tuesday after work. I'm painfully aware that we
don't fit the vibe as Sam and I check in at the desk of Smash
Point Social. It's been years since I felt like a fish out of
water, but when a woman walks out of the bathroom, her
hair pulled up into a high ponytail, her skirt and tank top
crisp in white and blue, my lungs struggle for oxygen.

I glance down at my oversized T-shirt and soccer
shorts. Not my best moment, but with a portfolio collapse
this weekend, I didn't exactly have time to wardrobe shop.

The sound of plastic balls hitting paddles, floors, and
probably walls assaults my eardrums while I try to understand what the teenager behind the desk is saying to us. He
wears a hat with the Smash Point paddle logo, his hair
curling around the bottom edges.

"Fifteen-dollar drop-in fee, or you can purchase a
membership and save—"

I smile and hold up a hand. "I called yesterday. I

purchased a semi-private lesson series with . . ." I check my phone to confirm the details. "With Frank."

"Oh, got it." The employee peers at one of the four computer screens facing him. "Yep, there it is. You're on court three." He points to the back corner, and I thank him.

"Were we supposed to bring balls?" Sam clutches her twenty-dollar paddle we picked up at Dicks on the way over. We stopped right after work and changed in their restrooms since I didn't want to be seen like this in the office. I'm wondering now if we should've listened to the guy who was trying to sell us on carbon fiber. Our paddles appear to be about half the thickness of the ones people are using on the courts we pass.

"I think they have balls," I say.

Sam snorts, and I nudge her shoulder. "Stop. This is a respectable establishment. We can't be—"

A man with a shaved head wearing a white undershirt from the nineties slams into the fence next to us.

"Oop, almost got it." He points to the yellow ball now bouncing between the courts. Sam rushes to catch it before it rolls back to the check-in desk, then tosses it over the fence. The man salutes, then turns back to the group on the court, shouting, "Six to two, I'm a one!" and smacking the ball from the baseline with a grunt.

Sam raises an eyebrow. "You were saying?"

Okay, so maybe I need to chill out. These people all look approachable. Maybe this isn't like the tennis clubs I grew up with. Plus, if they named the sport pickleball, they had to know that dirty jokes were on the horizon.

I scan the courts on either side of us as we walk the last twenty feet to court number three. Most people play in groups of four, and there's a good range of ages. Comforting, considering how my dad reacted when I told him I was taking lessons. *You're young. Play tennis now while you still can. Pickleball is for after you get a hip replacement.*

Then my eyes land on a man standing on the court across from ours. He's tall, obviously athletic, though I can only see him from the back. His calf muscles flex as he shuffles and smacks a ball with a loud pop, then moves back and gets in position for another one from the ball machine positioned on the other side of the net.

His strokes are smooth, strong. The ball whistles in a perfect arc, nearly grazing the net and hitting deep in the back corner of the court. I don't know much about pickleball, but it feels like that's what it should look like when it's done well.

He hits one into the net and growls something under his breath, then smacks his paddle against his thigh.

"Someone takes himself a little too seriously," I murmur, then jump at the sound of my name.

"Hey! Alecia and Sam?" A man with a kind smile and salt-and-pepper hair wearing an official navy-blue Smash Point T-shirt and black shorts waves us over to the fence at court three. "I'm Frank." He puts out a hand, and we each shake it, introducing ourselves.

Frank pushes open the gate, nudging the cart full of balls to the side so we can enter. "Hang your bags there, and water bottles can go in the corner."

I nod and hang my purse on the hooks, noting that everyone else seems to have bags with hooks on them. They're hanging directly on the black chain link fences surrounding the courts.

"I didn't bring a water bottle," Sam hisses.

I set mine down on the floor. "You can share mine."

She wrinkles her nose, and I laugh. "It's not like I lick the nozzle." We don't say it, but we both know she'll be removing the lid and waterfalling.

"Alright," Frank says, clapping his hands. "Welcome to Smash Point. We'll start with the basics. Today is a dink day." He grins, like he's waiting for us to comment. I mean, he did say "dink."

Sam keeps her mouth shut. I can almost feel the energy building from her internal struggle.

I clear my throat and point to the line at the top of the court. "That's up by the net, right?" I did some research the night before, so the word isn't completely foreign.

Frank looks pleased. He has smile lines around his eyes and mouth, and I can't help but think of my grandfather. "Good, Alecia. Dinking is the soft game. It's like flirting with the ball. No big swings. We're just getting to know each other." He laughs at his own joke and twists his paddle in his hand. "We'll talk about the rules of the game a little later, but for now, let's warm up."

He walks toward the net, and we follow. The court smells like acrylic coating, and I suddenly feel nine years old again, holding a tennis racquet that's almost as big as I am. There's that thrum in my chest, the rush of adrenaline.

"Let's stand at the non-volley line." Frank points to the thick white line running parallel to the net. "Sometimes called the kitchen line. You can't volley—hit the ball out of the air—while standing inside of it. You can step in the kitchen to play a ball that bounces, but then you'll want to step back out as soon as you can."

I nod and get my paddle into position, but Frank appears at my elbow. "Let's try this grip." He rotates my hand. "Continental. Like you're shaking hands with the paddle."

Sam and I both do the handshake as Frank rounds the net to face us on the other side of the court. "Soft knees," he says. "Paddle out in front. Think 'gentle hands,' a little looser grip. The goal is to drop the ball over the net and into their kitchen so it bounces low. Make your opponent hit up. Ready?"

I glance at Sam. She's already sweating. If she weren't holding her paddle, I'm pretty sure she'd be giving me the finger.

Frank rolls a ball with his sneaker, pops it to himself, and floats it over the net. I stab at it, and the ball hop-skips off my paddle into the bottom of the net.

"Perfect," Frank says cheerfully. "That's exactly what ninety-nine percent of tennis players do. Try this," he says, demonstrating a tiny lift with his wrist, like he's tossing a bubble. "Use your legs a little, and keep the paddle face a touch open. Meet the ball out front."

"Yeah, Alecia. Meet the ball out front," Sam murmurs, and I snort. She's not cracking jokes a second later because a ball comes to her next, but she does get it over the net in a tall, rainbow arc. "I did it! Did you see that?" She turns to me with a look of complete joy.

I laugh and sink into my knees, remembering what a ready position feels like. When I was sixteen, Dad strung a net in our driveway so I could practice volleys against the garage door. I wore a groove in the concrete and made our garage look like it'd survived a horizontal hail storm. "Gentle" wasn't part of our vocabulary.

Frank sends another soft ball. I keep the paddle face open, hold my arm out, and let the ball land on the face. It bounces off like it's a marshmallow, flutters over barely skimming the net, and lands on the other side.

"Yes," Frank says, satisfied. "Do that again a hundred times."

Sam and I hit ball after ball, and by the end of fifteen minutes, I'm hitting perfect balls over the net. My legs scream for a break, and Frank must notice our heavy breathing, because he sends us for a drink.

"Okay," Sam grunts and picks up my water bottle. "You didn't tell me we'd be doing twenty-minute wall sits."

I laugh. "Your next party trick?" I wait for my turn with the water, wiping the sweat from my face onto my T-shirt. With the smaller court, I wasn't expecting to get much of a workout, but my stomach's already grumbling. The protein bar I ate in the car isn't cutting it. I pull out a cinnamon almond butter bar and chomp it down.

After taking a drink, I turn and pause. Frank's talking with someone over the fence, and I put two and two together since the court across from us is now empty.

Ball Machine Guy nods and grabs his paddle from his bag hanging on the opposite fence, then walks through the gate onto our court.

"Wow," Sam says on a breath, and I shoot her a look. Yes. The man isn't unattractive. He's built like a swimmer, broad shoulders and a tapered waist, tan skin, and hair with a little curl that looks sun-kissed.

But his face is pulled into a permanent scowl, and his jaw is tight. He looks like someone who'd honk at an old lady who paused too long at a stoplight.

"Ladies, this is Calder. One of the pros like me here at Smash Point. He's going to help us with a little drill." Frank motions for Sam to pair up with him across the net, which leaves me partnering with Calder.

Oh, goodie.

"Transitions," Frank says. "You two at the baseline.

We'll be at the kitchen. Your goal is to drop the ball into the no-volley zone."

Sam whispers, "Ten bucks says I get a compliment before you do," and prances to the line opposite Frank. The little skank.

I itch my cheek with my middle finger, then turn and say, "Hi. I'm Alecia."

Calder nods once, then rolls me a ball under the net with his shoe. "Serve."

I bounce it, breathe, and do an underhand serve. At first, it looks nearly perfect, then it lands against the net and rolls back to me in slow motion. "Sorry."

His brows pinch, but he doesn't respond, just stands there waiting, not even preparing to hit the ball. Like he's sure I'll screw it up again. Meanwhile, I hear, "Excellent, lean into it a bit more, and that will be a perfect shot," from Frank next door.

I hit the ball. This time nearly sending it over his head.

"Too high," Calder says, smacking the ball back to me.

I can't help myself. "Oh, really? Looked great from here." I snap the ball back with a thwack, and it flies low over the net, taking Calder off guard. He throws his paddle up, but the ball skids and hits his knuckle. He curses under his breath, then jogs over to grab the ball now bouncing at the baseline.

Frank leans over the net. "Try to take a little speed off of that, and it should drop right on that line. Excellent work, Alecia."

I give Sam a self-satisfied smirk, then turn back to Calder. "Sorry about that. Thought you were ready."

Calder stares at me a moment, then hits the ball deep enough, I have to shuffle back. Oh, he's pissed. That sends a thrill through me.

After I successfully send three balls in a row into the kitchen—a beginner miracle—Calder starts hitting it harder. I can't help but pop it up, and he makes a show of lazily patting it back into the court. Sweat runs a ticklish path down my spine, and my shoulder's aching, but I refuse to ask for a break.

Frank finally forces the issue, and I stalk to my water bottle. Calder stops next to me and pulls his from his bag on the opposite side of the fence.

I take a swig. "Do you teach much?"

Calder gives me a look, but before he can answer, Frank does. "Calder's working to get his coaching certification. He's been shadowing me, and now he just has to get his own coaching hours in."

Wow. This was him after shadowing Frank? He was going to need a hell of a lot more coaching hours.

I lower my voice. "Is teaching what you want to do?"

He frowns, dropping his water bottle back in his bag. "Why?"

Umm, because you look like you'd rather lie on a bed of nails than drill with me? I shouldn't say it out loud, but it comes out anyway.

His mouth opens, then closes, and I'm a little worried about what's going to happen to the ball he's gripping in his hand. "Not everyone can be Frank."

A sliver of guilt lodges itself in the tender spot beneath my ribs. "That was rude. I'm sorry. It's probably me who's the problem." It was the likely scenario. I was out of my element, bristling at everything. Competitiveness was only helpful when you had the skills to back it up. Otherwise, you turned into a self-aggrandizing jerk. I didn't want to be that person.

I set my water bottle down and start walking back to

my side of the court, but before I know what's happening, I'm ripped sideways and thrown against something warm and solid. The split second it takes me to process my change of location seems to stretch into slow motion. Calder's left arm is around me, his right arm stretched over my head, catching a pickleball that's screaming straight toward my face.

"Ball!" A voice echoes through the club, but Calder has already plucked it out of midair.

"You okay?" he asks, dropping his eyes to mine.

I find it difficult to focus. He smells like soft cotton and clean sweat. I'm so close, I can feel his exhale on my forehead. And his eyes. Holy hell, his *eyes*.

I nod, since words have betrayed me, and Calder slowly releases his arm. I shiver, the hairs rising on my neck. That felt dangerously good. To be held by someone, literally protected from a projectile . . . How had he gotten here that fast? Reacted so quickly?

"Can't lose that one! It's a Franklin!" The guy calls.

Calder mutters something under his breath and throws it to him. I march back to the baseline. Doing my best to hide my flushed cheeks.

"Has Calder worn you out yet?" Frank teases as I take my spot.

Well. I'm certainly breathing hard.

"Takes a lot of drilling to make Alecia tap out." Sam says, stifling a snicker.

I purse my lips.

Calder bounces a ball on his paddle. "Maybe her partners just aren't drilling hard enough."

My jaw drops. Did he just—? Is Calder making a joke? Or is he oblivious to the baller innuendo he just dished out?

Sam's eyes water, she's trying so hard not to laugh.

Frank chuckles. "Well, we've got the right guy for the job then. Calder will keep drilling until you can't walk!"

He was *definitely* not aware of what he just said. When Sam excuses herself to get another drink of water, I spin toward the fence, finding as many new muscles to stretch as possible to keep from looking at Sam's shaking shoulders.

four

SAM

> So. Did Calder drill you until you can't walk?

ALECIA

> YOU'RE A TERRIBLE PERSON

I've had hundreds of mornings where I woke up sore after a workout, but this feels like I got dragged behind a pickup truck. I wince as I shuffle to the bathroom like an eighty-year-old, then hiss air through my teeth when I drop to sit. Did pickleball activate muscles never before used in my glutes and inner thighs? Ugh, or my abs. My fricking triceps. Every piece of me is steeped in a lactic acid bath.

If I thought sitting was hard, getting up is even worse. I

wash my hands, then immediately drop to the floor to stretch. My hamstrings feel like brittle rubber elastics, and my hip flexors are solid knots.

I haven't felt trashed in a fun way since high school tennis, when Coach Prewitt used to make us run ladders while telling us we were "barely approaching our potential." It hurts so good. I'm both concerned about my level of accepted masochism and excited that we have another lesson scheduled for Thursday. Hopefully sans Calder. *What kind of name even was that?*

He didn't say more than a few single words for the rest of our drill session after dropping his drill bomb. Sam and Frank were having a grand old time laughing and chatting next to us, and all I had was the thwack of the ball on my paddle and my insane curiosity to keep me company.

The way he moved . . . Not only to catch that fly ball, but on the court. It was like he had more time than I did. There I was, rushing and flailing to get my paddle under the ball, but he was already in position for what felt like a full second ahead of time. Like he was waiting for the ball to come to him. It was the same even when Frank had us standing directly next to the net, trying to keep the ball bouncing between our paddles.

And once I noticed his eyes, I couldn't unnotice them. They were seafoam green. Pale and almost mystical, like the crystals I used to pine after as a kid in gift shops. They held magical properties, and I was convinced that if I held them in my pocket or wished on them, I'd see fairies or acquire a talent for spells.

Not Calder's eyes. The crystals. Regardless, it was weird that I was thinking about either one this much.

I rush to get out of my apartment since everything takes longer with my new mobility issues. Putting on pants? I feel geriatric. But shoes? Pure torture. It takes me five minutes to lower myself into the driver's seat.

The drive downtown is a blessed respite, the equivalent of collapsing on the grass after a half-marathon. I've never run one, but based on the YouTube videos, I'm pretty sure that description is accurate.

The sun blinds me as I step out of the parking garage, a sheet of white glare ricocheting off the tower across Seventeenth and straight onto my retinas. Denver switched from summer to fall overnight, it seems, and I didn't get the memo. I wrap my arms around myself to keep warm as I walk down the block, then shoulder my tote and weave into the stream of suits, backpacks, and athleisure making its way toward the revolving doors of our building.

The lobby smells like eucalyptus and printer toner, which feels poetic given we manufacture the second and my stress levels this morning require the first. Steel columns, bright planters, a mosaic of commuters' reflections in the polished floor. This is the stage set I walk onto every weekday.

My calves whimper as the elevator climbs. I probably shouldn't have worn any heels given the situation, but flats make my legs look like I share genetics with a munchkin cat. Two floors up I'm already bargaining with my quads. *I'll give you protein if you get me to the breakroom without sounding like a haunted accordion.*

I step off the elevator and angle for Sam's office before retrieving coffee when I almost collide with six feet of warm, button-up, rolled-sleeve competence and a biodegradable cup.

Garrett.

Hold me, please, is my brain's immediate reaction, and I stumble back as he emerges from the breakroom. The hall is wide and yet I became a Roomba heading for the only obstacle. *No. That is not what we're doing.* I mentally slap my wrist.

His coffee is a pale, muddy brown. Garrett likes a little brew with his oat milk. His cuffs have a pink diamond pattern today, and his hair shines from whatever product he uses. With the scruff on his jaw, he looks like a 2018 Jake Gyllenhal.

"Hey, Alecia." He smiles, which is dangerous for my cardiovascular system. "Saw your name on the pickleball night list."

Garrett is talking to me. He saw my name on the list. *Dialogue. Response. Be a functioning human, Alecia.* "Yeah!" I squeak while grasping my purse strap like a parachute handle. "You play?"

Do not let on you know exactly which days he plays each week, that you've memorized his brand of bag, and looked up the paddle he uses online.

Garrett chuckles. "I do. You're into it, too?"

"Correct. It's a fun sport. I don't—I mean, I dabble." I flail a hand, and my tote slides farther down my shoulder. *Fun sport?* That's more basic than saying I like maple doughnuts.

He shifts his weight, amused. "Dabbling's a start." Garrett's eyes are hazel. I hadn't ever noticed that before.

"I used to play tennis. So. There's overlap."

His eyebrows tick up. "Footwork transfer pretty well?"

I nod, though I have no idea if that's true since all I did yesterday was stand close to the net and try to have "gentle hands."

His lips twitch, and he taps his fingers on his cup. "Well, I guess I'll see you tomorrow."

"You sure will!" I sound like Harry Caray. Or at least Will Ferrell's depiction of him.

Garrett walks away, but I stand there for a beat, replaying every syllable with forensic precision. I just had a conversation with Garrett Davis. A real conversation, not about clients or projects at work.

I pivot toward Sam's office and make a beeline. When I enter, she's at her desk, glasses perched halfway down her nose, a high bun that solidifies her sexy librarian look. The walls of her office are a collage of color swatches and art she bought in Europe. Sam is who I want to be when I grow up.

"On a scale from one to I-can't-sit-on-the-toilet, how are your glutes?" she says without looking up.

"It's like you're living in my brain." I ease myself into the egg chair, making my arms do most of the work. "Also, Garrett just ambushed me in the hall."

Her head snaps up. "What?"

"Okay, ambushed is a strong word. He stood there with his coffee while I attempted to run him over, then stumbled over every word I said and acquired a nervous system disorder. But hey, we spoke more than two sentences!" I bite my knuckle for effect.

She buys in, leaning over her desk and propping her head in her hands. "And?"

"He saw my name on the pickleball list for Friday. I said I played."

Sam winces, and I backtrack.

"No, I didn't oversell my skills or anything. I tempered expectations."

We grin at each other, the air between us filling with the fizz of excitement that always comes from doing something naughty.

"Well. That's something." Sam straightens, adjusting her glasses.

"Certainly something." I draw a deep breath, forcing myself to focus on the actual reason why I'm here. "We have a ten a.m. with GoodBarrel."

Sam nods. "Did you finalize the mockup for the mixed-pack?"

"Here." I drag my tote up and produce a folder. "Three versions. Gold foil on A, spot UV on B, and C is the budget-friendlier one with a matte varnish. I changed the typography hierarchy so the flavor reads first."

She pulls the designs out, and her eyebrows rise as she flips through. "This is good." She taps a thumbnail. "The foil's going to make their logo sing."

I beam at her. This is our secret romance language. Pantone colors, foiled detailing, smooth, embossed ridges, or the way a good weight of paper feels in your hand. Few things in life are more satisfying than opening a box of perfectly printed invitations.

"Did you hear back from Harvest Gala?" she asks. "Programs, place cards, four-by-nine menus?"

I nod, running my hands over the soft upholstery of the chair. "Confirmed specs. They're deciding between linen and felt for the stock. I pushed them toward felt with a deckle edge. They were drooling."

Sam laughs. "Deckle edges are the red lipstick of paper."

"Say less."

We run down the list: a conference booklet some oil and gas company wants to be forty pages, but they only have a budget for twenty-eight, a restaurant rebrand sprawling across menus and coasters, and the GoodBarrel boxes that could actually make our quarter.

When we reach a stopping point, Sam leans back and

stretches. I tap my phone screen and see we only have ten minutes before our meeting.

"Okay, I'll get back to my office." I cry just a little as I grip Sam's desk to force myself upright.

"Perfect. I'll see you on the call. And also at work tomorrow."

I pause, my eyes narrowing. That was a weird statement. "Are we not going out for dinner tonight?" It's Wednesday. We always go for dinner on Wednesday.

"Oh, yeah, that too. I just meant—"

"You're being weird."

Sam scoffs. "I'm not being weird."

"What is it?" I ask. She has something she doesn't want to tell me. We've known each other long enough, we may as well be an old married couple. Which is how I know that if I stand there and stare at her, she'll eventually break.

"I can't make the pickleball lesson tomorrow," she blurts.

"What? Why?"

"My brother and his fiancée are coming in last minute. It's a whole thing. We're doing dinner, my cousin from the Springs is meeting us. I have to leave early and meet them in Aurora because apparently Uber is too expensive, and I'm the only one who knows where to park a Subaru in LoHi on a weeknight."

"Okay, I'll reschedule with Frank." It's an automatic reaction, and I second-guess it immediately. I don't want to go to Smash Point Social by myself, but I also don't want to miss the lesson. The first pickleball club night is Friday.

Sam shakes her head. "No, you go. Seriously. I'll still be there Friday."

"You only got one lesson."

She winks. "I don't have anyone to impress."

* * *

On Thursday, I walk through the doors at Smash Point, shivering as the air conditioning hits my skin. Nobody likes a warm gym, but it's getting cold enough outside this week that the low temperature inside feels a little excessive.

The club is hopping tonight. People stand and chat in the aisle between the rows of courts. A sign at the front desk says, "Check-in for the mixed round robin in front of Court 1." Must be some kind of tournament or something.

I peer over, trying to judge skill level while I wait to check in, when I lock eyes with a woman who looks like she just stepped out of Sports Illustrated. I about swallow my tongue. *Holy what?* Megan's here?

I chose Smash Point because of its location in the opposite direction from Garrett's neighborhood, which is east of downtown and only about a fifteen-minute drive for me. The goal here was anonymity. I didn't want anyone at work to know I was putting effort into this. But when Megan leaves her group of friends and rushes toward me, that bubble bursts hard.

"Alecia?" She slows on her approach, probably confused as to why I'm skulking behind the fully packed sling bag hanging off the shoulder of the guy in front of me.

I pretend to be inspecting the snacks in the cooler along the wall. "Oh, hey Megan. What are you doing here?"

Megan smiles and pulls me into a hug because, of course she does. "I saw your name on the list, but I had no idea you played here."

I shake my head. "I don't exactly play here. I'm just checking it out."

Her eyes widen, and I get the same pit in my stomach as

when I stopped at the table outside the library a couple of weeks ago because they were offering free cookies.

"Oh, you're going to love it here. Everyone is so friendly, and there are plenty of lesson options, open plays, and leagues for all levels." She glances down at my paddle with more pity than judgment. "You can reserve the courts ahead of time. They even offer guest passes with a monthly membership purchase. Ooh! Does Sam play too?"

First off, I give her credit for knowing that Sam and I are friends. I honestly didn't think she'd noticed either of us. Second, I have no idea how to respond to that. I'm usually the perky one in any given conversation, but Megan's energy is unmatched.

I swallow the anxiety of this getting back to Garrett and try to accept her bid for socialization. "Yeah. We actually came and did a lesson the other day. I really want to get her into it."

Not untrue, though it did give the impression that I'm further along in this sport than she is, which is absolutely a lie. I still can't remember how to tally points in this game, let alone make one.

Megan smiles with approval, and I feel oddly accomplished. "Oh, that's amazing!" Someone calls her name, and she holds up a finger just as the man in front of me moves out of the way. I'm up for check-in.

"Are you here for the round robin?" she asks.

"Nope. Just here for a lesson."

The employee at the desk is the same one Sam and I met on Tuesday. I'm about to give my name when he says, "Alecia Monroe, I've got you on court three again."

I blink. That's twice people have remembered who I was tonight.

"Who's your instructor?" Megan asks.

"Frank," I start to say, only to have the employee jump in.

"Actually, Frank got himself into a pickle the other day. Strained something in his knee. He'll be out for at least the next week. Possibly six if his doctor gives him bad news."

Was that part of the training? They had to use "pickle" in everyday conversation?

Megan sighs. "Oh, Spencer, make sure to tell him I'm so sorry to hear that. Actually, you know what? I'll just post a message on the group chat."

Spencer smiles and moves on to the next person in the line while Megan pats my arm, tells me to have a great lesson, and jogs back to her friends, who are not so patiently waiting for her next to the fence of one of the courts.

Frank injured himself? Why didn't I get a notification about this?

I meander toward the aisle leading to court three and check my email. I only have to scroll down a few messages to see the one from Smash Point. *There's been a change to your lesson.* I click on the email, still walking as it loads. It's fine. I'm sure every instructor here is as good as Frank. I can roll with the punches. Be flexible.

The status wheel is still spinning when I reach the bench. I set my bag down, blow out a breath, and look up.

A man stands inside the fence with a basket of balls on wheels. Even from here, I can see I was right about the color of his eyes. Definitely liquid aquamarine.

Calder.

five

CALDER STANDS at the kitchen line, dark hoodie sleeves shoved to his elbows, dribbling a ball with his paddle. He looks up, and the thought of aborting the mission flashes through me with such intensity that my stomach yanks.

What am I going to do? Turn and run? Rude. Also, I paid for this, and I only have one more night before I'll be standing on the court with Garrett Davis.

"Hi!" I force myself onto the court with my sunniest expression. I don't know why he makes me feel like my organs are rearranging themselves, but I'm sure once we get into the drills, I'll get over it. "You and me again."

Calder's expression doesn't change. "Frank's out." His tone is lower than I remembered, almost creamy and smooth. Like he took a nap earlier and just woke up, a little groggy, and then I'm imagining him waking up in crisp sheets. He doesn't wear a shirt because *why would he* and—

"Ready?" He's pointing with his paddle to the other side of the net, and I'm not sure how long I've been frozen, staring at his pecs.

My brain is far too visual for my own good. I clear my throat and bounce past the post. "Sorry."

He nods with no "You're fine" or "No need to apologize." Just, "Start at the kitchen line."

Fine. This would be simple. Just like last time we could talk or not talk for hours. I almost snort, imagining that line in Jennifer Coolidge's voice. At least I can always entertain myself.

My first few dinks are objectively terrible. I know that now after watching an hour of pickleball YouTube with Sam on our lunch break. I send the ball high, and Calder, with very gentle hands, pushes the ball back to me. I breathe, bend my knees like Frank told me, and try to push, not swing.

"Bend your knees," he says.

I smile. "Yep." Okay. I *was* bending my knees, but maybe he couldn't see that through the net?

"Lower."

My legs are still sore from Tuesday, and it feels awkward, but I sink deeper into my knees, almost missing the next ball.

"Good."

That word sends a flash of heat down my spine, and I instantly bristle. *Red flag, A.* This is why I need Sam here. I need her to shoot me a look or something, remind me that I shouldn't feel so pleased by the fact that I gave him what he wanted.

But I can't help it. Ever since I was a kid, exceeding people's expectations was my own personal dopamine button. I could press it whenever I wanted. Do extra research for my project, and I'd ride the high from that surprised look on my teacher's face for weeks. The problem was, in high school, that turned into cutting my hair because Oliver Weld liked it short or never wearing pink because Jesse M. said it clashed with my auburn hair.

In college, it was giving up carbs because Aaron Foster liked women with six packs and then giving up my friend group because Max Cooper didn't like that they were so demanding when he just wanted to spend time with me.

So. Yeah. *Red flag, A.*

All the nervous energy makes my hands shake, so I do what I always do to get that feeling out of my body. Start talking.

"I signed up for lessons because there's a pickleball club starting up at work."

Calder blinks like he just remembered I was here. "Hm."

"Yeah. I think some of the people I work with are pretty good. But it's an open invite, so I'm assuming there will be other beginners."

"Lift with your legs, don't swing."

I nod. "Right. Okay." I try to do what he's describing and feel like I'm playing whack-a-mole. This has to look ridiculous, but Calder doesn't comment. The ball hits the net cord, and I hustle up to grab it and restart.

Calder motions for me to move cross-court before sending it back, and my brain lights up with the challenge. "Where should I try to hit it?"

"In the kitchen."

I purse my lips. *Obviously.* I laugh like he just made a joke and didn't sound like a complete patronizing ass. "Right, but where in the kitchen?"

"Not there," he mutters as my ball lands wide, past the line.

I straighten and plant my hands on my hips as he chases it along the fence. I could let it go. I normally would, but this is a pickleball instructor. A substitute instructor at that. Someone I never have to see again, if I don't want to. If I can't stand up for myself to him, then who *will* I be able to stand up to?

"Why not there?" I ask, my breathing quicker than it should be, considering how little work Calder thought I was doing.

"Gives too many angles."

I nod, still trying to be pleasant. "Yeah. This is my second lesson. Ever. So I'm just asking questions because I don't have any idea what the goal is." I didn't say, *And you're the teacher so you should know that and not treat me like an idiot*, but I hope he reads the subtext.

Calder hesitates for a beat, then points at the center line. "For now, when you're dinking, the goal should be to get the ball back to center. To reset. Try not to give them shots where they can be offensive and instead force them to make a mistake."

I smile. *See? That wasn't so hard.* "Thanks. That's helpful."

A muscle in Calder's jaw jumps, and my mouth goes dry. It's unfortunate he seems to have zero social skills because he's truly quite the specimen. And at least once was capable of making a joke.

I start telling a story about him in my head. How he was shy as a child, then got super hot and was traumatized when women had competitions to sleep with him. Or his dad was like Mr. Agassi and forced him to play pickleball for hours in the backyard when all he wanted to do was work at an ice cream shop or make hemp bracelets on the beach. My annoyance immediately dissipates when I imagine this poor, beautiful man being so unfairly treated.

He sends the ball back over the net, and I hit it with too much force. That's the most difficult part. The ball is hard plastic. The shots are similar to what I knew playing tennis, but I can't seem to figure out the power I need to hit it with.

Back to center. That was the goal. I blow out a breath and start again. "How long have you worked here?"

Calder hits the ball back low at my feet, and I barely get my paddle on it. When I do, the ball shoots high and lands past the kitchen line on his side. He grabs it and tries again, not answering my question.

The silence is torturous.

"You don't like to talk about yourself?"

He frowns. "This is a lesson."

"It is. But are you really going to *drill me* and not say anything for the next fifty minutes?"

Calder coughs, then clears his throat. "I've said things." His voice is hoarse, and I grin. I made him choke on his spit and that brings me pure joy.

He sends another ball to my feet, but this time, I miss it on purpose. "Wait!" I hold up a hand and crouch down, dropping my paddle onto the court. A large, gray spider is hunched there next to the kitchen line. I almost smooshed it with my shoe.

"What are you doing?"

"There's a spider." I move my paddle closer, hoping it will climb on, but it jolts in the opposite direction. "Shhh," I say, moving my paddle to the other side. I lay it flat, then move my hand behind the spider this time.

"Just kill it."

I look up at Calder in mock horror. "He's literally just existing. Why would I kill him?" I was the kid who moved snails off sidewalks after storms. Who kept earthworms from sizzling on the asphalt. How in the world someone could kill a helpless creature, regardless of how many legs they have, is beyond me. Calder is basically a monster.

My strategy works, and the spider bolts onto the paddle. I yank it up so he can't sprint off the other side. "Just a sec."

Calder watches as I leave our gated court and jog up the aisle to the front door of the club. I drop the spider in the planter out front, then reenter the building and hustle back.

"Okay, where were we?" Now I'm panting.

Calder's expression is unreadable. He looks at me, then at the net, then says, "Let's do a different drill."

"Fun." I position myself across from him, my feet wide. I refuse to let his attitude get me down. I'm going to learn some pickleball and enjoy myself on this Thursday night, damn it.

He glances down at my paddle hand. "You shouldn't be using that."

"Now you tell me."

Calder's jaw ticks. He stalks off the court, and for a moment, I wonder if the whole spider rescue broke him. When he returns, he's holding a sleek black paddle with a blue wrapped grip. "Here."

"For me? It's beautiful."

He's holding a breath. Completely exasperated. Besides my four-sentence conversation with Garrett, this is the highlight of my day.

"Just try it."

I give a heel kick and get back to the line.

After only a few shots, I realize the new paddle is life-changing, but I'm not ready to admit it. Every hit feels like it pops instead of dying on my paddle if I don't hit it dead center.

Fifteen minutes later, we're practicing backhands. He has me stand directly next to the net and lean over, isolating the motion. Calder feeds me balls, and I swing my arm like a pendulum to hit them against the wall. I get bored after hit number five and commence babbling. " . . . and GoodBarrel approved the foil, which is probably the fastest any company has ever approved a proof. And then Friday we have a company pickleball night."

"Less wrist. Just move from the shoulder." Calder reaches out and adjusts my arm. My next words die on my tongue. His hand is warm, his palms a little rough.

"Got it." The words come out breathy. How long has it been since I was this close to a man I wasn't related to? You know, besides being whisked into his arms the other day to avoid pickleball shrapnel.

The thought sends me down a spiral of patheticness. No, there was that date I went on. The guy who was friends with Sam's brother. It was a complete bust, but he did hug me after the show. That counted. Even though it didn't have a smidgen of the effect on me that Calder's right hand just did.

I panic. "There's this guy at work who plays pickleball. Kind of why I'm doing this." He doesn't ask me to go on, and yet I do. "I figured if I took lessons, I wouldn't look quite so terrible at our company pickleball night."

"This is for a guy." It's a statement, not a question.

My cheeks flush. "Yeah. He's . . ." How would I describe Garrett? "All around impressive."

"You're into him?"

Wow. After not piquing his interest for the last half hour, this was the topic that did it? "Well, I am picking up a sport for him. So . . ."

I hit the ball in a perfect, smooth motion. "Hm. That was good." I compliment myself since he won't, and his lips twitch. It was almost a smile, and I lock in right then on my new mission. Break Calder by the end of the lesson. I may not be his cup of tea, but this is a public service. I can't release him out into the wild to terrorize other helpless pickleball amateurs without giving it a solid college try.

"No notes. I'm an expert now," I declare after hitting the last ball in the basket. Calder hands me one of the ball-collecting tubes. I set my paddle on the ground and start next to the wall, the balls making a satisfying thunk as I drop the cylinder over them, forcing them into the chamber.

Another instant game. Beat Calder with how many balls I can collect. "I win." I dump my first tube full into the ball basket.

He grunts. "Not a competition."

"You're only saying that because you lost." I grin and start with the next gaggle of balls near the back fence. When I fill up a second time, I turn to see Calder walking faster than he needs to with his tube and note the location of the basket. "Not fair. You moved it."

He shrugs and dumps his balls in. "Only saying that because you lost."

My smile splits my face, and I can't help it. I laugh out loud. It's the second thing he's said that proves he isn't a pickleball robot, and it makes me giddy. *Did I lose?* I don't think so.

A thousand questions fill my head, and the fact that he won't answer any of them makes the itch of curiosity that much worse. Why doesn't he want to talk about himself? He's secretly a pro player and doesn't want anyone to figure out his true identity? He's in witness protection? His ex works at the pickleball club across town and he's raising a pickleball army to beat her at nationals?

I smirk at the possibilities when a woman walks past the court and waves. "Hey, Calder!"

He gives a polite smile, and she blushes.

Ooooh. Yeah. Now I get it. He acts this way because he doesn't want women to get attached. I mean, *look at him.*

I suddenly feel sheepish. How many women has he coached who show up hoping for an after-hours drill session?

But he doesn't know me. That I'm obviously taken. Futuristically.

When I'm standing next to the basket, I make a show of emptying my tube. "Sorry I pried. I won't ask any more personal questions. But you don't have to be so serious all the time. I think this is supposed to be fun."

Calder hesitates, observing me for a moment, then takes the tube from me and hangs it on the fence next to his. "I finished clean up while you were distracted."

Mm. It's the small victories.

six

IT'S FRIDAY AFTER WORK, and my whole body buzzes as I wait for Sam to change in the locker room of the pickleball club. The vibe is opposite of Smash Point, and I'm already judging it. Didn't know two lessons could build loyalty, but all the chrome and black, plus the heavy bass that makes me feel like I should be wearing a mini skirt or at least a thong, makes me antsy.

If Smash Point is Instructor Frank, then this place feels like Calder personified.

It's a bummer we won't be going back. Smash Point had a great vibe, but we only had one lesson left in the packet I booked with Frank, and since he was definitely going to be out for a couple of weeks, he sent an email apologizing for zero notice on the switch Thursday and offered to refund me.

"Did you bring an elastic?" Sam emerges from the changing stall. I hand her the one from my wrist. At least once a week, she's in need of a little hair support.

Sam and I push through the locker-room door into a narrow hallway that opens to the courts. The ceilings are lower than Smash Point's. The lights are brighter, too, and there are only three courts in one row. Past the back wall there's a tiny lounge—a handful of bar stools, a glass cooler with canned seltzers, craft beer, and energy drinks. A chalkboard sign says, "Have a ball, Paper and Pixel!" which is kind of adorable, but very much not on brand.

We gather near the others. I recognize Megan and Garrett, of course, and a couple of other people from the design team. I clock people from different floors—prepress, sales, accounting—including a quiet, moustached man I've only ever seen on the elevator and a woman from bindery who once sent Sam and me cookies at Christmas.

My nerves set in as Megan raises her hand to get everyone's attention. What was I thinking, believing I could pick up a sport in a week and a half?

Breathe. *You wore the cute skort.* The goal was never to be the best, just not to be laughable.

When nobody stops talking, Megan whistles and calls, "Alright, team!" Ten heads swivel. "Welcome to week one of Friday Night Pickle," she chirps. "We'll keep it fun and fair." She points with a paddle. "We'll rotate partners every game so we can all get to know each other's style. No two fresh beginners on the same team, and court one will be the winners court. You win, you stay. You lose, you hop to the next court down."

Winners court. Okay, that makes me want to barf.

Megan continues, "If you're newer, start on courts two and three. If you're feeling spicy, try court one. If you don't know a rule, ask! We're here to have fun." She seems to finish, then remembers, "Oh! And first drink is on Pixel and Paper!"

The group cheers at that.

Garrett calls out, "Also, you may have noticed our odd

number. I invited a friend to make us an even twelve. He should be here any minute, so start your warmups and we'll be good."

"Damn. I was hoping I'd get to sit for a game." Sam folds her arms in front of her.

I put an arm over her shoulders. "You're the best for being here."

"You're booked for Oktoberfest."

I snort.

"Hey, now we know Garrett has friends."

She gives me a look. "Was there ever any doubt?"

"Just sayin.' Seems like a green flag."

Sam laughs as we walk toward the courts. We hover like twin satellites waiting for some group's gravity to pull us in as pairs begin to form around us. I avoid looking Garrett's direction. Don't want to make it too obvious, plus it's probably better if I play my first game with someone else.

"I guess we should split. Two newbs." Sam glances toward court three.

"Probably." I don't like it but she's right. I drift toward court two and see Garrett jog through the gate. He runs past me and slows at the front, greeting someone who—

Oh. My. Hell.

Is that—?

Sam calls my name, and I turn to see her nod toward the entrance. I mouth, "I know!" then turn back to make sure my eyes aren't deceiving me.

Nope. It's him, alright.

Calder walks past the front desk with Garrett. He's in a dark T-shirt and shorts, his paddle bag slung across his back. Garrett says something, and he huffs a laugh. It's only a small smile, but the sight of it tightens a knot in my chest. *He looks like a normal guy.* Yes, still a bit serious, but not nearly as buttoned up as he was at Smash Point. Was he like that because of his job? Or was he in a pissy mood because of me?

He scans the room, cataloging people, courts. When his eyes land on me, they widen. He blinks, then drops his gaze and hangs his bag on the fence.

This is Murphy's Law. Absolutely impossible. There are a million people in this city, and *he's* the friend Garrett invited to play pickleball tonight?

Sam is suddenly next to me. "He knows Garrett?"

"Apparently." I already filled her in on my lesson with *not* Frank.

Megan leaves her court and runs up to greet Calder with a hug. He stands there and takes it, doesn't even lift his arms, then nods and says something I can't make out from here. Not sure what to make of that, but I don't have time to speculate because I'm already freaking out.

They must know each other from Smash Point. Or did Megan know him before she started playing there? Were they—?

"Are they together?" Sam asks.

That thought should've sent my body through the roof with excitement. If Megan was with Calder and Garrett was Calder's friend, then he wouldn't be trying to sleep with her. Unless he was a complete asshole. I guess it wasn't completely out of the realm of possibility, but he didn't seem that type to me.

But if he wasn't trying to sleep with her, then was I completely off? Had I missed a cue in Garrett's body language? And why was there a pit in my stomach instead of a pink bubble of happiness?

It had to be my own ego. Megan knows I was at Smash

Point, but now Calder knows this is the company I work for. *And didn't I tell him I had an office crush?*

I groan and turn my back on them. "He knows, Sam."

"Knows what?"

"I was all nervous, and I babbled about tonight. I told him I was learning pickleball to impress a guy—"

"No."

"Yes!" I hiss, taking a play from Garrett's book and pinching the bridge of my nose. Why do we do that? It's not like putting pressure on my nasal passages will make this any less embarrassing.

I don't wait to find out if Garrett will call my name or if I'll magically end up on the same court as him. I grab Sam's arm and yank her back to the court she came from with a breezy, "Mind if I hop in?"

The man from sales—Jerome?—opens his palm with a flourish. "Be my guest. What's your DUPR?"

I blink, frozen like a deer in headlights. Sam doesn't seem to have a translation at the ready either, so I ask, "DUPR?"

He gives a self-satisfied smile. "It's a ranking system for pickleball. To show your level of play."

I laugh. "Oh, well, then I'm probably whatever the lowest number is. Zero?"

Jerome shakes his head. "I doubt that. But you should play with me. Megan will be back in—"

"Perfect. You found a partner." Megan pushes through the gate. "Jerome and Alecia against Sam and me." She hops over to the other side of the court, and I pray I look even half as good as her in my tennis skirt.

My heart pounds so fast, I'm lightheaded and jittery. What was I thinking? I barely know the rules to this game —haven't even played a game with a partner. But, I remind myself, most of my favorite things in life came because I ignorantly jumped into something. Including Sam and my current job.

Jerome spins his paddle. "You want to serve, or should I?" He's lanky, mid-thirties, and he's wearing black socks with dill pickles on them.

"You serve." I stand dead-center at the baseline of the right-side box.

Jerome walks closer and waits a second. "We have to switch spots then."

"Oh! Right. Of course." I pretend I understand that even though I don't. Note to self. Sam stacks across from me, holding her paddle at her side. I motion for her to bend her knees and hold it out a little. Ready position. Calder drilled that into my head at our last lesson.

Jerome calls, "Zero-zero-start!" then smacks the ball with his paddle. It flies over the net in a clean, low arc. I do know where the serve needs to land, at least. In the opposite box.

Sam swings and misses, and Megan claps a hand against her paddle and says something I can't hear over the plinking of plastic.

Jerome and I swap places, and he calls: "One-zero-two."

Perfect, okay. We have one point. Because we're serving and they missed it.

On the second serve, we aren't so lucky. Megan returns the ball with a smack, and it comes straight toward me. I move into position, my footwork rusty but coming back from my tennis days, and promptly slam the ball into the net.

"Definitely not a zero." Jerome chuckles behind me. "Just get lower and that'll be a killer drive."

I nod, then grab the ball, not sure what to do with it.

"It's their serve. Whoever starts only gets one chance to serve, then from there on out, each person on the team gets a turn to serve," he explains.

I give a grateful smile and toss the ball to Sam. She looks nervous, but her first serve goes in. My palms are sweaty. I draw a deep breath and take a little more time getting into position before my swing. This time the ball sails over the net.

I let out a cheer of surprise, and Jerome has to yell at me to get up to the kitchen line. I can't wipe the grin off my face, even when I miss a shot and they tie up the score.

This is fun. It's fast-paced and unpredictable. My brain lights up recognizing patterns with the ball and trying to coordinate my out-of-practice body. Even though I'm awkward, Jerome and I find a rhythm.

He's good and more than makes up for my poor decisions. No matter what they hit at him, he seems to get it back. Not as smoothly as Calder, but it's effective. We win 11-6, and when Megan and Jerome approach the net, Sam and I follow. They hold out their paddles, tapping the edges against each other, and we join in.

Adorable.

Megan brushes a stray lock of hair from her face. "Okay, let's see who else is finished and we'll switch it up."

I wince. "But Jerome—"

"You don't get to keep him, Alecia," Sam says, and Jerome gives an "Awe shucks" wave of his hand.

Megan rounds the net. "You two did great for just starting. Have you played another racquet sport before?"

Sam shakes her head, but I nod. "Tennis."

Megan picks up her water bottle from the floor beneath her bag. "No wonder. Some of those shots you hit were tough."

The compliment feels like a warm hug, and I feel the teensiest bit less self conscious around her. When she leans over to replace her bottle on the ground showing perfect cleavage, my progress evaporates.

"I'm going to go fill up," I say, leaving the court and grabbing my mostly full water bottle from the backpack I used for my trip to Europe two years ago. It doesn't have a hook to hang on the fence.

I hurry to the water fountain between the restrooms, and stutter step to a stop when Calder turns, his water bottle in one hand, the lid in the other. "Oh. Hey."

I glance to both sides, searching for an escape route, but the women's bathroom would still require me to move closer to him. My only option would be to turn around and bolt. I'm half considering it when he says, "So." He doesn't move, still blocking me from accessing the water fountain.

I wet my lips. "So. You're friends with Garrett Davis."

"I am."

"How long have you known each other?" I ask, then think better of it. "You know what? Never mind. You're not going to answer me anyway."

He screws on the lid to his bottle and finally steps to the side. "This isn't a lesson."

I scoff, stepping up and putting my water bottle under the filler. "Seriously?"

"I like to keep things professional."

"Okay. Because having friendly conversation isn't professional."

He blows a breath through his nose as my water bottle fills. "I've known Garrett since last summer. We partnered together in a tournament."

I take a swig of water, then top off the bottle and screw on the lid. "Well, if you wouldn't have been so *professional* in our lesson the other day, we could have avoided all this awkwardness."

"What awkwardness?"

I give him a look. "You're going to pretend you don't remember what I said?"

"Oh, I remember."

The way he says that makes my stomach flip. I clear my throat. "Yeah. Then you understand why this is the seventh level of hell for me." I walk past him.

"A little dramatic."

I whirl. "What?"

"Seventh level of hell?" Calder scrubs a hand over his jaw. "Seems like a bit of an exaggeration."

I step closer and lower my voice. "Just forget everything I told you, okay? Play the strong and silent type. You're good at it."

"You think I'm strong?" He gives a half smirk.

I groan and stalk back to the courts, praying he's only trying to piss me off and isn't going to word vomit all this to Garrett.

Somehow, I end up playing with Jerome again. We win a close game, moving us into the middle court. We have to split and play with the losers of the top court, and my knees go weak when I see it's Garrett and Lisa from accounting. I glance over and see Calder with his partner waiting for the middle court winners. It's Megan and her partner. Of course it's Megan.

Garrett gives me a half smile as he approaches. "Looks like it's me and you."

I hope the blush rising to my cheeks looks like athletic effort. "Looks like it." I smile, but my insides are now inside a Vitamix that is cranked up to the soup setting. I won with

Jerome, and Garrett seems better than him. All I have to do is minimize mistakes. Breathe, stay low.

Garrett shades his eyes with his paddle. "Want to start serving or receive?"

He's smiling at me. Garrett Davis is maintaining eye contact, proposing we engage in a physical activity together, and *smiling at me.*

I'm a genius. I wish Sam were standing here because she would know this exact look on my face and find some way to bring me back down to earth. All this time I thought it was skincare and pilates that were the key to attracting men, but turns out, it's a pickleball membership.

"Receive," I say, because the idea of serving right now makes me queasy. The ball would fly into the back wall with the adrenaline pumping through my veins right now. Plus, Lisa's the one serving. Not nearly as intimidating as Jerome. As long as I stay opposite her for the entire match, I might not have a panic attack. Technically that's impossible, but still.

Lisa calls out 0-0, and her serve zips. I return it cross-court, and when Lisa sends it back toward me, Garrett slides a half-step in front of me and takes the shot, feathering a drop into their zone.

I rush forward to the kitchen line, but Jerome sends the ball to my knees, and I can't get my paddle low enough before it bounces through my legs. Fantastic. Not embarrassing at all.

"Nice try, Alecia!" Jerome grins and waves his paddle. I roll my eyes. He has no idea I'm a total beginner, and I don't expect him to give me special privileges, but we just played together. He knows my weaknesses.

Garrett holds out his paddle, and I tap it. Not a big deal. It was one shot, and at least I returned the serve respectably. Jerome and Lisa switch spots so she can serve to Garrett.

"Let's get it back," Garrett says.

Lisa serves to him, and he smacks the ball to Jerome, who immediately sends it my direction. My paddle's up, but it doesn't matter. The angle's all wrong, and the ball flies straight up.

Garrett turns his back to the net. "He's targeting you."

"Yeah, I noticed." I grit my teeth, trying not to imaging slamming the ball into Jerome's crotch. Can't he see I'm trying to impress a guy here?

Lisa's next serve comes straight at my body. I manage to send it back, and Garrett intercepts the counter. He spins a sharp drop right into the corner, and we snag a point. 2–1. We're rally scoring, which is both exhilarating and stressful. Every point counts, and we can't let our guard down.

I plant my feet wider, try to remember to keep my paddle out in front, higher closer to the net, and a thousand other things, and for three whole rallies, I hold my own. My returns stay low, my resets land where they're supposed to. We get ahead, 4-3.

Then Jerome starts aiming lower. Faster. They go up 8–5 before I blink, and I hate this. I don't know why I ever decided to pick up a paddle and sign that stupid form. Now, instead of just being the girl across the hall, I'm the girl across the hall who sucks at pickleball and who Garrett probably hopes won't come back.

I'm not a person who struggles with negative self-talk, but standing on that court with my palms sweating unlocks the door to my inner critic.

We score a couple more points, but so do they. It's 10-7, and they're serving.

My nose burns as Jerome serves and Garrett returns

deep. I drop to my ready stance, and Lisa pops it back to me. I step in, bend my knees, swing—

Too much.

The ball arcs, and I know what's coming before Jerome even moves. The smash echoes across the court. Pain blooms sharp and immediate in my thigh where the ball connects with bare skin just below the hem of my dress. A red-hot sting radiates outward, and my breath catches.

"Oh, shit, Alecia, I'm so sorry."

I force a smile that feels like stretching with a sunburn. "No, it's fine."

"I was aiming for your feet." He runs a hand over his buzz cut.

My eyes sting. Tears start to blur my vision. Maybe if I were a pretty crier, I wouldn't worry so much about showing emotion in public, but I'm not. I'm a puffy-eyed, snot-nosed, blotchy-cheek kind of girl, and I'm not going to allow any of these people to see that over a stupid welt from a ball.

"I'm going to hit the restroom," I chirp, then rush off the court. I drop my paddle on the bench and jog toward the hallway. Inside the restroom, I lift the loose fabric of my skort and check out the red mark blooming across my thigh.

The sting is already starting to dissipate. I slip into a bathroom stall and pull out a handful of toilet paper to blow my nose. It's a game, it isn't a big deal. It didn't even hurt that bad, it was just shocking, and I can't keep my eyes from watering. I just need to—

"Alecia?" a male voice barks, echoing off the tile.

My mind races. Do I recognize the voice? Hard to tell since the sound is all distorted in here. Could it be Garrett? My heart races, and I clear my throat. "Yeah?"

The bathroom stall door rattles. "Let me see it."

I toss the used toilet paper in the little trash can next to the tank. Not Garrett. The voice is too gruff. But who would follow me into the bathroom? "I'll be out in a second."

"Your feet are facing backward. You're not on the toilet. Just open the door."

I scoff, my eyes flashing. He was looking at my feet? I whirl, flick the lock, and yank the door open. "Listen, I—" I freeze. Calder stands in front of me, his jaw tight. His hands on his hips. His eyes drop to the red, angry mark on my thigh that looks a little like Swiss cheese, I guess because of the holes in the balls. Before I can protest, he leans down and wraps his hand over my thigh.

seven

I SUCK in a breath at the flash of cold, and I must stumble because Calder grabs hold of my arm. "What is that?"

"Ice pack."

I blink. I can't see anything under his hand. "I'm fine."

"It will help with the swelling."

"I doubt it'll even bruise."

His eyes flick up. He lets go of my arm, but keeps his hand in place on my leg, crouching so he doesn't have to bend over, and my mouth goes dry.

His face is directly in front of my stomach, and I have the sudden urge to reach out and run my hands through his hair. His thumb slips against my skin, and my stomach lurches.

"Here, I can—" I put out my hand, motioning for him to let me hold the ice pack against my own skin.

"Oh. Right." Calder hesitates, then straightens and hands me the ice pack. He steps back and looks a little dazed, bumping into the sink before backing up toward the door. "Just wanted to give you that."

"In the women's bathroom?" My pulse is still rushing through a crazy straw.

"Uh, yeah. I . . . wasn't thinking." He scrubs a hand over his jaw, but doesn't leave.

"Thank you."

He nods once. "Okay."

"Okay."

And then he's gone, ducking through the door. What just happened? Calder was in here barely thirty seconds after I was. He was playing on the winner's court wasn't he? Had he left his game for this? Did he think something worse had happened? That I'd gotten hit in the face?

Maybe he was a medic or a doctor for his day job. Maybe his life was so stressful treating patients in the hospital, pickleball was his only way to unwind. And I treated him with such disrespect.

I hold the ice pack on for a few more seconds, then slip it into the pocket of my tennis skirt and march back toward the courts. I don't want anyone to think I'm upset, but I'm not worried about looking it. Any tears threatening to escape were shocked back into my body the second I saw Calder on the other side of that door.

Court one is empty, and there's a group of coworkers laughing and drinking, gathered around a table with high stools. I seriously debate joining them until I see a three-some, including Sam, waiting for me on court two. Garrett's on the top court with Calder. Guess it doesn't matter that we lost?

I grab my paddle and apologize for the wait, showing off my battle wound. My new teammate is an accountant named Josh who reminds me of an antelope when he moves for the ball. A little jerky and bouncy at the same time. We rotate partners twice, and at some point, I have to rally with Sam. It feels unfair. We both started at the same time, but I have years of tennis experience to draw on. I try not to hit it too hard, but Sam is going all out, and by the end of it, she and I are laughing so hard we can barely stay upright.

By the time our court bookings are up, my calves ache, I'm soaked in sweat, and the ice pack has melted to a lukewarm blob in my pocket.

The group trickles off the courts, people chatting and joking around. I sit on the bench by the court, pull off my indoor shoes, and stretch my legs, sighing with the release. It really is more work than I thought. Mental and physical. Half the time I miss points it's because my head is out of it, not my body. In tennis, I have more time to react. More buffer. With pickleball? I have microseconds.

After slipping my sandals on, I glance down the aisle and see Calder packing up by himself. No Garrett. I scan until I find him leaning on the counter at the front desk, laughing with the staff.

I grab my backpack and shoes and walk over to Calder. "Are you a doctor?"

He stares at me. "Because I carry ice packs?"

"No, that's—no." I compose myself. "It made more sense than you just being a nice guy."

Calder huffs what sounds very much like a laugh. His eyes meet mine, a smirk still playing on his lips, and something about the weight of that look makes my pulse trip. He follows my motion as I pull the pack free, and heat rushes straight to my cheeks.

He takes it slowly, fingers brushing mine for a fraction of a second. "Definitely not a doctor. Not a nice guy either."

"Nope. Your cover's blown."

He flips the pack in his hand, then walks over and drops

it in the trash can. All while maintaining eye contact. My face flushes hotter. It's a single use ice pack. Of course it was a single use pack. Why would Calder have a frozen reusable ice pack in his bag?

"I'm an idiot."

"You say that a lot." He slings his bag over his shoulder.

I frown. *Do I?* "Really, I just wanted you to throw it away. So I don't have the personal guilt of ruining the planet."

Calder just stands there, watching me. I back up and drop my gaze. "Well, thanks for the help. I wish you the best of luck with your pickleball . . . stuff." I turn, desperately searching for Sam to give me an easy out from the cherry on top of my most awkward night ever. *I gave Calder my warm, used, disposable ice pack.* Ugh.

"You're not doing more lessons at Smash Point?" Calder asks.

I shake my head, scouring the area outside the washrooms. Sam is probably changing. *Hurry up,* I silently plead. "No. Frank refunded me for the last lesson we booked."

Another pang of sadness hits my chest. It was fun playing tonight. Less fun partnering with Garrett because I couldn't stop worrying about what he was thinking, but that was my fault, not his. I did want to get better, but signing up with a different club and starting over again sounded worse than reliving my last blind date. It involved a man who ordered milk with dinner and asked if I believed in chemtrails.

Garrett's laugh sounds from the front. He says something and turns to walk back toward us, smiling like he has a secret. I decide to stay put instead of hustling to the bathroom, just in case Garrett's things are in the bag still sitting on the bench. Maybe we can chat while he packs up.

"It's him."

I flinch, my head whipping back to Calder. "What?"

"The guy you're trying to impress."

I make a sound in my throat, already sweating again. "What? No. He's not—"

"So it's Jerome? Or Josh?"

I open my mouth and close it. I had a choice to make, and neither option was pretty. Admit I was into Jerome with his mustache and sleeveless shirt, or Josh who was at least four inches shorter than me, or admit the truth. "It's J . . . erome."

I made a decision and height won out. It was the wrong choice, based on the expression on Calder's face. I'm instantly in middle school again. *Do you have a crush on him? Circle yes or no.*

Calder glances at Garrett walking closer, and his brows pinch. "I need coaching hours at Smash Point to finish my certification."

"Okaaay."

"You could take lessons there. From me."

I laugh. "Do you not remember our last lesson? Pretty sure that was your personal Hadestown. Not an exaggeration this time."

His frown deepens. "I thought it went well."

My eyes widen. "See, now I'm concerned. If you thought that went well, what do your worst lessons look like?" When he doesn't respond, I worry I've hurt his feelings and backtrack. "It's not that the lesson was bad. I learned a lot, actually. You just seemed miserable."

He grunts. "Because I wasn't chatting and saving arachnids?"

I scoff. "No! Because you seemed allergic to my personality!" I school my features. "Sorry. It's just that when humans make expressions like this," I grimace and hunch my shoulders, "It usually means they aren't in love with their life choices."

"That's my normal face."

I laugh. "No it's not. I saw you on the court tonight."

"You were watching?"

"I—no. I just happened to notice you didn't look like you were about to pass a kidney stone."

"Hey!" Garrett appears next to us, throwing an arm over Calder's shoulders. "Looks like you two are talking about something juicy."

I sigh. "Just waiting for Sam." She still hasn't left the restroom, and I'm starting to worry she got stuck in a stall with no toilet paper.

"Did you get to play together?" Garrett asks.

Calder shakes his head, and I say, "Didn't make it to the winner's court."

Garrett laughs. "Yep, that's where he was parked all night. Mostly because of Megan, though, right?"

I bristle, then remind myself I literally started this sport a week ago. Of course Megan's better than I am. It was a miracle I could play at all.

"You made it to the middle court, though." Garrett smiles and shoves his paddle in his bag.

I sigh. "I did. And then made you lose."

Garrett chuckles. "They were using some off-brand balls. If we had Franklin, we would've been fine."

Calder's jaw tenses, and he mutters. "It's never the balls."

"What?" Garrett grins.

"Ah, nothing."

"Thanks for waiting." Sam nudges my side and hands me my elastic. I slip it over my wrist.

I grin, the world settling back into equilibrium now that she's here. "Shall we?"

"Please."

I turn back to Calder and Garrett. "This was fun."

Garrett nods in agreement. "Have a great weekend."

"Will do!" I link arms with Sam and we walk to the exit.

"He complimented you," Sam hisses as we step out to the street.

"What?"

"Garrett. I heard him when I walked up. He said you made it to the middle court, and it was the ball's fault."

I bark a laugh. "That's not a compliment."

"Absolutely was. He could've said it was all your fault you lost, but he didn't. First of all, he claimed you as a team member by using 'we,' then insinuated he made mistakes too, which means, by default, that you didn't make all the mistakes and must've done some things right. So. A compliment."

I'm grinning at her. "You're my favorite person."

We debrief on the drive home, and by the time I drop Sam off at her apartment, I'm wiping tears from my cheeks, I'm laughing so hard.

"Maybe a little shaming is good for us?" I call out the window.

"Speak for yourself!" She flips me the bird, as she should, and walks into her building. Apparently, while I was playing with Garrett, she'd tripped over her own feet and done a half somersault in front of Josh and one of Megan's friends on the design team. I didn't see it, but my mind is more than making up the difference. My version is definitely the best version.

I arrive home, find a spot on the street, and take the stairs to the second floor. When I first discovered this apartment three years ago, it was beyond affordable. But gentrification in the neighborhood is jacking prices everywhere. Not that I'm complaining. It's incredible to have a cute coffee shop, a Trader Joe's, and a farm-to-table restaurant all within walking distance. But my rent is going up two hundred dollars a month in the new year. Sam and I are in negotiations for upgrading our relationship to roommate status.

I throw my backpack on the couch and grab a fork along with the container of chicken salad I made Wednesday. I scoop bites directly into my mouth, then eat a mandarin orange, grab a wine cooler, and head for the shower.

Peeling off my sweaty clothes and stepping under the scalding water is heaven. I stand there with my eyes closed, letting the water run over my skin until I'm no longer chilled, then pop open my drink and sip. I've never been happier with myself for not making any weekend plans. Sam's Oktoberfest extravaganza is scheduled for next Saturday, which means I can get a little buzzed, sleep in, catch up on a project or two, and spend Sunday afternoon with my parents.

My mind flits back to Garrett. His comment at the end of the night hadn't even phased me. Probably because I was so distracted thinking about Sam and living the awkwardness that was Calder.

Why was he so strange? Was there something about me that brought it out in him? He seemed to communicate fine with Garrett and the others, even Megan. They played together most of the night. *Was I the problem?*

No, back to Garrett. We had more interactions tonight than in a week at the office, but had they accomplished anything? Was there any sign he was interested?

I didn't understand how he worked. That was the problem. He was so driven and focused. I needed to figure out what got him outside of that ambition and competitiveness. To slow down and notice what was right in front of him.

I use the grapefruit scrub Sam got me for my birthday and wash, finish my drink, then step out and towel off. It's only ten. Plenty of time for a face mask.

The collagen film is cool and slimy as I pull it out of the packaging, but it feels amazing on my skin as soon as I get it in place. I moisturize, comb out my hair, and wrap up in my plush, ankle-length robe. Time for Bridgerton. The new season dropped at the beginning of the year, but I only watched the first episode before my nights were swallowed up with work trips and my annual Mother's Day cruise with my mom. Then summer hit, and I hadn't gotten back to it. But this weekend was perfect for binge-watching.

I find my phone on the counter and settle on the couch, my head pleasantly fuzzy. While Netflix loads, I check my texts and email. Just a few promotions, a message from my bank about enrolling in e-statements, which I thought I did weeks ago, and—

I frown. There's an email with Smash Point Social in the subject line, but it's not from Frank. It was sent five minutes ago, and the sender's name is Frederick? I click on it.

Hey. Got your email from Frank. If you're interested in lessons at Smash Point, let me know.
   Calder

I blink, rereading the message. I only had one wine cooler, so this wasn't something I was making up. Calder emailed me? He got my email from Frank? Frank looked like he'd be in bed at eight o'clock at the latest, and most disturbing, Calder's real name was Frederick?

I click reply.

Hey, I'm so sorry, I think you might be looking for someone else. I don't know a Frederick.
   Alecia

I grin and click play on episode two, but keep my phone out. Calder sent that message recently enough, I secretly hope he sees my reply and responds. I straighten when the bolded message blinks into existence.

Thought you were smart enough to make the connection considering the signature.
   Calder

The idea of him sitting on his couch, a scowl on his face, makes me chortle. Does he think it's funny or is he actually pissed? He must really need these coaching hours if he's messaging me at ten o'clock on a Friday night.

Oh, Calder! Right. I owe you a single-use cold pack or $0.67, whichever value is greater. Would you prefer Venmo or Paypal?
Alecia

My pulse rushes. I don't know why I'm messing with him, but it's too fun to stop. I should've eaten more chicken salad because the cooler has obviously hit me harder than expected.

His reply is almost instant.

It was branded, so closer to $1.13 but no need to reimburse. Flush in cold packs at the moment.
So no lessons?
Calder

I snort. What was it about these lessons? Was he going to ask me for ten friends who might be interested in a new and exciting opportunity?

Right. I get that you're desperate. I'm sorry you can't find anyone to sign up for lessons with you, though I did give you feedback that I hope you're taking into consideration.

I pause and rethink that. He seems to be playing along, but will that offend him? I delete the sentence.

Right. I get that you're desperate, but we haven't discussed compensation. What's in it for me?

I stop the show because I have no idea what's happened in the last eight minutes. My eyes are glued to my phone screen.

I thought free lessons were in it for you.

My eyes widen. I hit reply.

Oh, free? See, that was an important detail you failed to mention.

I laugh at the ridiculousness of this. We're emailing like I used to in elementary school—bypassing the school system to message before I was allowed to have a phone. The thought occurs to me that I could give him my cell number, but I push it away. He's a pickleball instructor with gorgeous eyes who happens to know Garrett Davis. We really have no reason to contact each other.

Another message comes through.

> *Thought it was implied. I need coaching hours.*
> *Calder*

I adjust the edges of my mask, then wipe the excess product on my neck before typing back.

> *Seems like I'm doing you a favor here. It's a bit of a drive to Smash Point. I might need you to sweeten the pot.*
> *Alecia*

I second guess it the moment I send the message. It wasn't meant to be debaucherous, but I read it from a man's perspective and send a quick addendum.

> *That was a joke. Not me implying anything. Just ignore. Sorry, had a wine cooler and I'm in a robe.*

I press send and groan. *I told him I was in a robe?* Okay, new rule. I have to count to ten before my thumb hits the blue button.

It takes a full three minutes before he replies, and I'm

sweating bullets, probably negating any benefit from the collagen soaking into my face.

That explains a lot.
        Calder

I immediately break the rule I just set for myself.

Which part?

The TV screensaver comes on, but I barely notice.

The robe, obviously. Only people with trust funds and emotional support pets lounge around in robes on a Friday night.

I snort. I'd worn robes since the time I was nine. They were my preferred late-night pajama wear because when I was ready for bed, I could rip it off and get under the covers.

Tell me more about how your parents didn't love you, I send back.

That would drastically cut into your beauty sleep.

Something twinges below my ribs. Was he kidding? Regardless, that response sobered me.

Maybe you could buy me some of your favorite balls.

Both times someone mentioned loving or hating pickleball balls, he got all testy. I have to know why.

I don't have favorite balls

Ha! I laugh and write back, *But I thought the type of ball you play with really matters?*

That's a cop out. Good players can play with any ball

I reply, *Just making sure I'm reading you right. Seemed like a sore subject*

. . .

He doesn't respond right away, and I worry I've angered the beast. I send another message.

> *Let me talk with Sam about the lessons. We were kind of supposed to do it together. Really appreciate the offer.*
> *-A*

I wait a few moments, and I'm just about to put the phone down and restart my episode when a bolded message jumps to the top of my inbox.

> *Have you figured out Garrett yet?*

My heart jolts. I sit up straight and hunch over my phone.

Is there something to figure out? I type, not exactly sure how to respond to that. This was very not professional.

> *You said you were into him.*

Um excuse me, I never said that. I keep reading.

We've been friends for a while. I could probably give you some tips.

My cheeks warm, my whole body tingling. My thumbs start to type.

Trade? I help with your coaching hours, you help with . . .

I pause, trying to figure out how best to say that. *With bagging Garrett? With convincing Garrett to love me?* I laugh. Nope.

You help me be more attractive to men?

Well, one man specifically. I press send. At least it's funny. The idea of having insider information about Garrett makes me feel a little dirty . . . and I can't say I'm opposed to it. Sam is going to lose her mind when I show her screenshots.

His response is instant.

Deal. Sam's welcome, too.

eight

THE NEON PADDLE sign over Smash Point Social blinks as we cross the parking lot, trying not to blow away. Sam and I parked next to each other. It would've been ideal to drive together, but she has to leave ten minutes early to get on a family video chat. Her brother's planning a wedding, and she's doing the invitations.

I shiver, wishing I'd brought a better jacket. The wind picked up after work, and now the black clouds are rolling in with it. The Tuesday night air smells like fall leaves, rain, and smoked meat from the taco truck sitting at the back of the parking ot. My stomach wishes we'd arrived a half hour earlier.

Sam bumps my shoulder with hers. "What secrets do you think he's going to dish?"

I groan. "I have no idea. This is a bad idea, right?" Who am I kidding? Even if we had shown up earlier, I couldn't have eaten tacos. My stomach has been in knots since the weekend.

"I don't know. He's the one who offered."

I wince. "Meaning what? That he won't tell Garrett?"

That was the "what if" keeping me up at night. What if this was all some stupid set up? What if Garrett had seen me salivating, peering at him through my office windows, and thought it would be hilarious to play a game with me?

I think of Calder bringing me the ice pack. Of Garrett closing deals at work. Did I think either of them were capable of something so mean-spirited? No. But the insecurities inside me aren't quite so confident.

We step inside and the familiar Smash Point soundtrack envelopes us. Paddles kissing balls, sneakers squeaking, the playlist bumping 90s hits. Cool air slinks under my skirt, raising goosebumps along my thighs.

The lobby and open spaces between courts are surprisingly packed. People cluster around high tops, laughing and sharing food.

"Is this some kind of event?" Sam murmurs.

I look for one of the signs we saw last time, but don't find anything, so we weave to the front desk. The girl with space buns and razor-winged liner blinks up at us. "Hey! Court reservation?"

"Lesson with Calder." I almost call him Frederick for fun. I didn't tell Sam about that. Huh. Not sure how that slipped my mind.

Space Buns tilts her head. "Calder's in the round robin right now."

My stomach does the cartoon-fall-through-a-rug thing. "Did I mess up the day?" I mutter to myself, hunting for my phone in my bag.

"Hey!" Someone yells, and all three of us look up. Calder leans over the fence, his paddle in hand. He yells again, and I don't catch the first part, but I do hear, ". . . check your email?"

I whip out my phone and tap on my inbox. Frederick sits at the top, and I thumb the message open.

Round robin's running late. Finish in 30ish, then I'm yours. Sit by court two.

 -C

My heart does a stutter step. *Then I'm yours?* I blink and shake my head. That was a common turn of phrase. I press the screen against my hip. No need to read that over again. "Looks like it will be a few more minutes. You good to wait?" I ask Sam, and she nods.

Space Buns smiles. "Perfect, so drop in fee or—"

"Erin! Don't charge them. I'll explain later!" Calder leans over the fence closest to us. He waits for her acknowledgement, then jogs back to the baseline. The group of people at the table next to the court look over in curiosity. Perfect. We're attracting attention.

"We can pay." I reach for my wallet, but Erin shakes her head.

"Nope. Calder's got it figured out. He'll help me take care of it. Just give me your names."

We do so, and since we've been there before, our waivers are already in the system. We end up on a row of stools next to court two, shoulder to shoulder with a knot of people who are already shouting at Calder and his partner like this is the US Open.

A woman with curly red hair offers us a paper tray of sweet potato fries. "You new?"

"Kind of? Just starting lessons. Alecia. This is my friend Sam."

Sam gives a wave.

The curly-haired woman grins. "I'm Natasha. That's my husband, Ben." She points to a tall, easygoing guy who's got a toddler on his hip using a paddle like a drum. "We're the unofficial Smash Point peanut gallery. We heckle out of love."

A guy in a vintage Nuggets tee leans in. "I'm here for the snacks." He takes a fry and Natasha swats at his hand.

Another woman—platinum bob, glossy lips—opens a cooler bag. "We've got seltzers if you want one."

"I—sure," I say, taking a can and handing one to Sam. Cold condensation hits my fingers, and the tension in my chest unkinks a degree.

"Who are you cheering for?" Ben asks. "You got a horse in this race?"

"Uh, our lesson is with Calder."

The group hoots like I announced a celebrity crush.

Natasha leans in. "Ben says I'm not allowed to have real people on my hall pass, but Calder's on it."

"What is she saying?" Ben fights off the child in his arms who's currently trying to reach inside his mouth. "It better not be about the damn hall pass."

Sam snorts.

"You haven't bought any skorts yet, babe," Ben says, returning to the table.

Natasha rolls her eyes. "Oh, don't start."

"Calder is into them. That has to be your first move—"

"*You're* into them, and I don't have the thighs for that. We've discussed this," she snaps back, and their conversation devolves from there.

Sam and I exchange delighted smiles and try to focus on

the game. As the play heats up, the chatter is replaced by reactions to the shots. It gives me a second to sip my drink and watch.

Calder is different when he plays. Not that I have much to compare against, but just with the three other people on the court, he looks smooth. Seamless. He's playing with a woman in a neon visor, Kari, according to Tasha's running commentary, who prowls at the net and loves to hit hard. Watching her gets my blood pumping.

That's the kind of player I want to be. Aggressive. Not afraid to go for the ball.

After three points in a row, I notice a pattern. Calder sets up points like puzzles. He serves it deep, then hits the return ball at the feet of whichever player is farther back in the court. He and Kari adjust position depending on who the ball goes to. It's like they're tag teaming, and it's super effective until the guy on the other team flips a perfect lob over both of them. Calder has to run back to hit it. He returns it over the net, but the other woman slams it at Kari's feet.

Calder taps paddles with his partner, gets back in position, and then stills.

"Kari coaches Saturdays," Natasha says. "Really nice person. Never want to play her, though."

Ben adds, "She body bags like nobody's business."

I glance at Sam, and she shrugs. At least I'm not the only one who has no clue what that means.

We fall into cheering with the others. Giving teasing groans when someone flubs, appreciative "oohs" when Calder threads one down the line. Between points, the group adopts us wholesale. Sam tells them we work in printing and design, which immediately sparks a debate over cardstock vs. linen. A woman behind Natasha is printing graduation announcements, and somehow that leads to my confession that I once cried over a deckle edge.

By the time the game hits 8–8, I know Natasha's kid is named Junie, Ben hates pickles, platinum bob's name is Myra and she runs HR at a tech startup, and Nuggets Tee is actually named Marco and prefers filing his taxes in February so he can bring it up as much as possible in March when everyone's stressed.

I've never felt so at home somewhere I've only been twice.

"Side out!" someone yells, as Calder's team takes the serve.

He and Kari creep up from the baseline with smart drops. The rally has me on the edge of my seat, especially when Kari smashes it only to have it come straight back. Damn, these people are good.

Kari gets a dink that hits the net cord and drops into the kitchen, and the other team can't get it in time. 10–8. Game point.

The other team buys one more chance to serve, but Calder and Kari hold them. They take eleven with an ace serve by Calder.

"They got third!" Ben says to Junie, brushing his nose against hers.

Oh. This was an actual tournament. "How often do they do these?"

Natasha shrugs. "Usually something competitive every week. These are just our in-house tournaments. We only have the big hosted ones every few months or so."

Calder, Kari, and the other team all tap paddles over the net. Calder says something that makes the other guy laugh, and when they walk off the court, everyone is all smiles.

"Alright, time to get this little one to bed." Natasha takes Junie from Ben. "Gah, I'm sore."

Ben laughs. "Weird. You only played for five hours today."

"Five hours?" My jaw drops.

Natasha laughs. "Someone needed a sub in Net Queen tonight. We never have enough women—ooh! You two should come sometime!"

I draw in a breath. "Is that—are we allowed to come?"

Marco slings his bag over his shoulder. "Are you members here?"

Sam and I shake our heads.

He waves it off. "No worries, just talk to the front desk to add you for the day. I think it's a fifteen-dollar drop-in fee or something."

"But you should obviously buy a membership so we can play together." Natasha winks. "We have events almost every weekend, singles meet-ups." She waggles her eyebrows. "Not that I think you're single, I'm just saying you'd both do well there."

Ben chortles. "What does that even mean?"

"What? It means they're young and cute!" Natasha smacks him with her free arm, then adjusts Junie on her hip to grab her water bottle.

Calder's making his way over, and he looks stupid hot. His skin glistens, his shirt clings to his toned chest.

When my pulse rushes, I turn back to the group and hop off the stool. "We'll definitely look into it."

Sam quirks a brow. My voice was a little too high, and even I heard it. "I'm nervous," I murmur, just to make sure she knows that's all this momentary weirdness is. Because that *is* all it is.

"You ready?" Calder asks. *Was his voice always that low?*

I spin and nearly hit Junie with my bag. "Oh my gosh, I'm so sorry!"

Ben laughs. "You had inches to spare."

Calder looks between Sam and me. "Sorry to make you wait." He unclips a towel from the side of what must be his bag hanging on the fence and wipes his brow. His phone sits in the side pocket.

"Here." I point to it and hold out my palm.

He freezes. "What?"

"Hand me your phone."

His brow furrows, but he pulls it out and gives it to me with the screen locked.

I sigh. "Open, please." I want to say something about how his phone would never recognize me because my face wouldn't do the whole permanent scowl thing, but people are still milling around us. I don't want to embarrass him.

Calder hands it back, open, and I tap on his contacts.

"This is so you can text me next time. I don't typically check my email outside of work hours," I say. He raises an eyebrow, and I give him a look. "Okay, that was an anomaly."

Sam's eyes narrow. "What was an anomaly?"

I wave her off. "Nothing. I just happened to see a message. About the lessons." My cheeks heat. Calder's eyes seem to bore into my forehead, so I focus harder on typing in my number since I seem to have forgotten the last four digits. *How long had we email chatted the other night?*

Giving him my number wasn't about that, it was practical. What if he'd needed to cancel tonight? I would've been ticked to drive all the way over with no notification.

I hand the phone back to Calder, and grab my bag, purposefully not watching as he reads his screen. I wasn't planning to write out my full name, but it only felt right after seeing "Frederick" in my emails. You show me yours, I'll show you mine.

Mabel Alecia Monroe. At least as embarrassing as his first name. Who names their kid Mabel? Did my parents expect me to come into the world loving polyester and hard candy? I may have teased him the other night, but I, of all people, know what it's like to grow up dreading roll call on the first day of school.

Calder catches my eye as Sam and I say our goodbyes to the disassembling group. He's still holding his phone. I expect him to look away, but he doesn't, so I laugh a little too loud at Ben and Junie, then ask, "Which court?" in Calder's general direction.

"Six," he says.

Calder hasn't warmed to me, which would normally be fine. However, this isn't a normal situation. I very much want him to give a good recommendation to his friend, but no matter what I do, it only seems to sour him further.

My heart is still racing after that look he gave me, but bringing it up now would be weirder than just letting it go. First my wine-emailing and now this? *Damn it.* He probably thinks I'm trying to hit on him or something.

I replay the woman walking past the court, then me asking for his phone. I should've said it more formally. Something like, "Perhaps I should give you better contact information so you're able to apprise me of any schedule changes." How many times had he told me he wanted to be professional?

"What's happening right now?" Sam whispers as we walk to the bench at court six and drop our things.

"Nothing." I smile. "Just thinking."

"About a pap smear? You look like you're going to crack a tooth."

I blow out a breath. "Calder isn't my biggest fan."

"What? That's not true."

I turn my back to Calder so he can't lip read. "He never smiles when I'm around, Sam. Watch." I grab my paddle and get on the court. As soon as Sam joins me, Calder herds us to the kitchen line.

"Dink warm-up," he says. "No swings. Thirty-ball rally."

"Oh, is that all?" Sam smiles sweetly, and Calder's mouth turns up.

That! Right there! He never does that to something I say!

I try to catch Sam's eye so I can throw my arguments telepathically. She doesn't notice since Calder is throwing her a ball, and she's wholly focused on tapping it over the net to me.

I did it again. Somehow managed to ruin his mood without even trying. The whole name thing was supposed to be a kind gesture, but here he was looking like someone just spit in his coffee.

Acknowledge it. That was the only option. If he'd gotten the wrong impression, I just needed to set it right.

"I think I bring out the worst in you," I say, shuffling to get the ball, sending it back to Sam.

"Me?" Calder's brows pinch.

"Who else? It's not Sam."

Sam grins. "Well, I wouldn't say that."

I scoff and hit a ball into the net. "You think I'm a bad influence?" I bend to get it, then toss it over, and drop back into my squat.

"Not a bad influence, just a . . . you know. An unrealistic influence."

I cackle. "What have I done that's unrealistic?"

"Oh, I don't know, believe you can pick up a sport in a

week and a half? Believe *I* can pick up a sport in a week and a half?" Her breathing quickens as she darts for a ball. It's not pretty but she gets it over.

"Pfft. Look at you. You *are* picking it up."

"Don't lean. Use your feet," Calder says, and Sam points as if to say, "See? Someone agrees with me."

Calder doesn't respond to my comment, so I double down. "How unrealistic do you think it is for me to get Garrett's attention?" We both know why I'm here. Maybe Calder just needs to be reminded that I'm solely focused on that goal so he doesn't make assumptions and get pissy.

"Garrett's attention isn't hard to capture," Calder says, and my jaw drops.

"Okay, ouch."

"I didn't mean it like that. I meant—"

"That he doesn't stay with women for long," Sam finishes. "We've covered that." She gives me a pointed look.

"Just because he hasn't stayed with someone for a long time yet doesn't mean it can't happen. People change." Hopefully with me and not Megan. "He's just been so career focused. You really can't blame him."

"Like *I* can't blame him? Or the proverbial you?" Sam asks.

I smirk. "Either, or both. Also," I turn back to Calder. "I hear you're into pickleball skorts."

His face reddens, but he plays it off. "Who isn't into pickleball skorts?"

"Well, we're both wearing them. And you haven't said a thing."

Calder rolls his eyes and focuses hard on the ball. After much effort, Sam and I finally string together twenty-one not-the-worst cross-court dinks before Calder finally gives us a break. Then he does some training on paddle angles. Wrists. Anticipating. Using our legs. I swear my brain will break playing this sport before my body will.

"Let's try seven-eleven," Calder says. "You and me. Sam will rotate in. Kitchen versus baseline. Your goal is to drop the ball into the kitchen and not give me an offensive shot."

"So you're going to smash it at me. That's what you're saying."

He shrugs. "You have control over whether I do or not."

I roll my eyes and take my place on the baseline. "You do remember I've been playing for a week."

Calder's eyes drop to my thigh where there's still the remnants of a blotchy pattern on my skin from the hit I took on Friday. "I'm not going to hit you."

His voice is soft, intense in that way that I'm realizing is uniquely him. It's like he's more tuned in than other people, but on a completely different frequency.

Calder taps his paddle to the net. "You only have to get seven points to win. I have to get to eleven."

"And what do we get if we win?" I purposefully say "we" so it doesn't sound flirty. But the fact that I have to think about it makes me realize *I want* to be a little flirty with him. Not because I'm into him, of course. He's like Mr. Darcy or Han Solo. Someone who needs a woman to kick them in the pants and get them to loosen up. Maybe if I could crack that thick shell of his, he'd realize I'm not some flighty party girl after his friend. After the ice pack incident, I know he has a softer side, and that's the side I need if I want an ally in Operation Garrett.

"You get the satisfaction of winning." Calder's expression is unimpressed.

"But I like prizes. Or treats." Okay, so that wasn't helping with my public image.

"She loves treats!" Sam plops on the bench between the courts.

Calder blows out a breath. "Fine. You can have a sucker."

I scoff. "There are suckers in the bowl at the front. I can already have a sucker."

He wets his lips. "Not if I tell them you can't."

The temperature ticks up a few degrees, and my head goes a little fuzzy. I swallow hard, then laugh off my sudden heat flash. "Fine. A sucker it is."

Damn, Frederick. He needed to save that banter for his girlfriend. Wait, did he have a girlfriend? "Are you dating someone?"

Calder serves the ball, and I do my best to reset it. It goes too high, but he doesn't take full advantage. Expecting a faster shot than what he sends me, I knock it into the net.

"This is a lesson." He scoops the ball under the net with his paddle.

"We've already crossed your weird professional line," I mouth more than say out loud. I wonder if he heard me over the music, but then he says, "No."

"No?"

"I'm not dating anyone." He sends the ball back.

I swallow my pride and try another reset, getting it a few inches lower. When I hit it into the net on the next shot, he calls out, "Two to zero."

Perfect.

"Why aren't you dating?" I ask.

"Too busy," he shoots back, serving me the ball.

"But that's in your control." I get lower and successfully get a ball to drop into the kitchen. I make a new victory noise that I swear has never left my lips, and Calder misses the shot. "Ha! New strategy!"

Calder doesn't look amused. "Why aren't you dating someone?"

I grin. "Well, I'm not *yet*, but I'm putting forth effort." I return the serve, sending the ball wide. Somehow he still gets it, sending it straight to my feet. I miss it and have to chase it back to the wall. "That's the problem," I call a little louder. "I don't get to choose whether I date someone or not. They have to agree to it."

"Preach!" Sam shouts.

"And we're told that all men want endless women, and yet all we see are men sitting at home by themselves. I don't even know what they're doing." I grunt as I hit the ball back to him, putting a little of my frustration into it. He has to jog back to grab it. "What are they doing, Calder?"

I was an attractive woman. Not like Megan attractive, but I had what Sam and I both agreed were good boobs. And that was the terrifying part. Maybe men were putting stock into personality, and they just didn't like mine.

"You don't want to know." Calder waits for me to get into position.

"I very much want to know."

"It would pop your little bubble."

My eyes widen. "My bubble?" I turned to Sam. Proof. Right there. "Do you think I'm—"

"Don't say idiot." Calder gives me a look.

"—oblivious?"

"You do seem oddly happy."

Sam nods in understanding. "I thought she was doing mushrooms or something. For like the first two weeks I knew her."

Sam and I met back when I was still at my old marketing job and she was the freelance designer assigned to one of our product campaigns. She barely hid her eye rolls the first few meetings, and honestly, knowing her backstory, I couldn't blame her. She was in the middle of the hardest year of her life. Her best friend from college had taken his own life a few months prior. Nobody saw it coming. My perkiness may as well have been a physical blow.

"If you can't beat 'em, join 'em." Sam shrugs, and my heart warms. Most people thought I was putting on a show, wearing a mask of toxic positivity. When Sam realized I was really just a squirrel with the attention span of a goldfish, we became fast friends.

With those positive vibes, I win two points. Only because Calder's trying to lower his game-play and it's throwing him off. The line of his mouth is more relaxed, and that feels like the highest praise. He beats me 11-4, then as Sam rotates in he tries to make me feel better by giving some spiel about how playing the baseline is more difficult. Another almost compliment. I'm beaming as I take my place on the bench, dead set on earning that sucker.

Sam cackles when she swings and misses the ball completely. "This paddle is too small! I need way more surface area."

Calder blows out a breath, his mouth curling at the edges, and a flash of jealousy curdles my stomach. *He smiles for her?* What does he have against me? Am I that annoying to him?

Sam only gets to three before he hits eleven and has her switch to the kitchen. Since she has to leave, we both agree she should go first. She manages six points that time, then wipes her brow and jogs over for a hug.

"See you tomorrow?"

I nod. "You did great."

She huffs. "Not a sports person."

"You're lying to yourself."

She grins and waves, then heads of the court. Now it's my turn to be the player at the kitchen line. Even though there are people all around us and Sam is still gathering her things at the bench just outside the fence, my nerves amp up having Calder's attention completely on me.

I adjust my paddle grip, then serve the first ball. It's a thousand percent easier to score points in this position, but Calder still gets back every ball I hit.

"To my feet," he barks.

"Yeah, I'm trying."

"Don't be afraid to attack it. Keep your—"

"Paddle up. I know." I grit my teeth and serve.

I put up a good fight, but he still beats me 7-10.

"I think you were actually trying on that one." I plant a hand on my hip.

Calder fiddles with the wrap on the handle of his paddle. "I'm always trying." His brows are furrowed. He won't even make eye contact.

I glance up at the screen on the fence. Two minutes left. Yeah, I'm done. "Thanks for the lesson." No code cracking for me tonight.

As I walk toward the gate, my brain finally clues in on the silence around us, and I turn to see all but one of the courts empty. "Wow. This place cleared out fast."

Why am I making small talk? For all I know, that's what sets him off. My inability to be silent like he is.

"Yep."

I set my paddle on the bench and take a swig from my water bottle. Calder walks to the corner of the court and retrieves a ball we neglected to pick up.

"Time to pay up."

He pauses at the gate. "You didn't earn the sucker."

A laugh bursts out of me. Seriously? "The tips, Calder. For me and Garrett?"

His jaw tenses. He nods once, then sets the ball in the holder on the back side of the wall, and exits the court. For a moment I wonder if he's going to admit he doesn't have any advice and only said that to get me and Sam to show up, but then he says, "He likes competition."

I chew my lower lip. "Okay. Like—"

"Garrett wants to win. He's always more interested if there are high stakes."

"Mm. Perfect. So I challenge him to a duel? Pistols at dawn?"

A corner of his mouth ticks. "Make him think there's someone he's losing to."

That makes it click, and it seems stupidly obvious. Of course. Men were always more interested in a woman who was desired by other men. "So I pretend to have a boyfriend."

He grunts. "That could work." Calder takes off his shoes and shoves them in the bottom compartment of his bag, drops the paddle into a back pocket, and puts on his slip-ons. "You walking out to your car?"

I nod, pulling on my sweatshirt. Guess I'm washing this. I didn't realize how sweaty I was until I stopped moving and the AC hit me full force.

Calder hangs his bag back on the fence.

"Well, I guess I'll see you . . . sometime." I sling my backpack over my shoulder.

"I'll walk you out."

"That's not necessary."

He peers at the dark windows. "It's late. I'm going to walk you out." He starts for the doors, so I don't bother protesting. I'm tempted to grab a sucker from the bowl as we pass the front desk, but don't out of principle. Even though Calder fabricated the stupid rule, it's annoyingly motivating.

We push through the inner doors, and when we exit through the storm doors to the parking lot, I gasp. Rain is coming down in buckets. There's a small awning over the entrance, so we aren't immediately soaked through, but the rain seems to be coming from all directions.

I laugh, remembering my car is at the very end of the row. Wasn't expecting a thunderstorm in early October.

"Do you have an umbrella?" Calder calls over the hissing rain and grumbles of thunder.

"Nope!" I grip my bag strap tighter and gear up to make a run for the back of the parking lot when I see it. Nestled along the sidewalk is the largest puddle I've seen in years. My eyes grow wide as saucers.

"What is it?" Calder leans in, peering through the sheeting rain.

I point. "That's insane!"

"Oh, yeah. Happens every time it rains. The asphalt is graded in the wrong direction."

I turn to face him, my eyes huge, a goofy grin painting its way across my face. I shouldn't do this. He already has opinions about me, but . . . that also means I have nothing to lose, right? And this puddle isn't going to last forever. "I'm sorry. I have to."

nine

I DON'T CARE that I barely know this guy. This is way too good an opportunity to pass up. And, I'd be lying if I said I didn't want to show off a little.

Being around Calder with his judgy looks and obvious disapproval of everything that is me, makes me intent on proving something. On standing up for every person in the world who smiles and dances for no reason. I need to prove that this way of living is better than his. That there is joy to be had in normal moments and people like him are missing it.

I shove my bag back against the doors under the awning. Calder gives me a puzzled look, but I figure at this point, a picture is worth a thousand words. I launch myself out into the rain, jumping with both feet into the massive puddle lake.

"Alecia, what the hell?" Calder lunges for me, grabbing my arm as I throw out my hands for balance. I didn't exactly calculate for the instability of my flip-flops, but that oversight is completely overshadowed as the cool water sends a shiver up my spine. It's impossible not to grin like a maniac.

I rotate my hand to grip Calder's wrist and tug. It's what I would do if this were Sam. He looks at me like I just tried to pull him head-first into a lava pit.

"Come on." I laugh, my hair slicking to my forehead. I don't know why I'm so intent on forcing him to loosen up, but once the idea catches me, I can't let it go. He just looks like he needs to belly laugh or get a massage or— I halt that train of thought on the tracks. "When's the last time you jumped in a puddle?"

"A long time ago. For good reason."

"What good reason? It's amazing." I slosh out to stand next to him, dirty water running in rivulets down my calves. Our hands are still wrapped around each other's wrists. "You wanna do it together?" He grimaces. "Come on. You're already wet."

"Whose fault is that?"

I scoff. My pulse rushing as his thumb shifts over my wrist. His hand is warm, his grip tight. I like the feeling a little too much. "I'm going again."

"You're going to fall on your ass."

I hold up our entwined hands. "You'll keep me steady." The rain pounds around us, blurring his edges, making everything soft. I crouch, give a few good pumps with my arms, swinging Calder's along with mine, then jump into the puddle a second time.

I throw back my head and laugh. It's the most ridiculous thing. Not the puddle jumping, but the fact that as we get older, we become so concerned with getting dirty or having to do laundry or clean ourselves up or be uncomfortable for a few minutes that we miss out on the simplest pleasures.

"You're insane," Calder calls out.

I drop his hand and throw my arms out, lifting my face to the sky. I spin in a slow circle with my eyes closed. "When I was a kid, I used to stand like this and pretend that I was the one who controlled the weather."

Calder's quiet and I peek a little. He's watching me, water running over his lashes. "Are you doing it right now?"

"What?"

"Controlling the storm?"

"No."

"Pretending?"

My grin stretches wide, raindrops falling into my mouth as I slap my arms to my sides. "But what if I *was* controlling it?"

"Wow."

I open my eyes to see Calder shaking out his hair like a wet dog.

"You're really missing out." I motion to the water that's at least half way up my calves. Now even more muddy since I've churned it up. Calder blinks rapidly a couple of times, draws a breath and holds it, then shakes his head and takes a step back. For a moment I think he's going to ditch and go back into Smash Point, but then he hesitates. The wheels are turning in his head, and I can almost see the moment he decides.

I squeal in surprise. "You're going to do it?"

"Don't make this a thing." He kicks off a shoe.

I'm so excited I can't figure out what to do with my hands. "No. I love this. Just be careful because you're not wearing any sandals."

"It'll probably be more stable that way."

"But there are rocks under here." I shift my feet and a few crude pebbles bite into the foam of my flip-flop.

Calder drops his shoes and socks next to my bag and turns barefoot, his hands on his hips.

I back up, giving him space. "Don't think about it. Just jump."

"That's not how I live my life."

"This is a very low-risk proposition."

It takes him a minute to work up to it, his toes flexing on the wet concrete. But when Calder leaps, he leaps. I half expect him to curl into a cannonball.

I shriek and turn away as the splash hits me, soaking me up to my waist. And when I turn to see Calder's expression, I can't stop laughing. He looks like a little kid who just touched slime for the first time. Both disgusted and a lot intrigued. I snort trying to catch my breath and clap a hand over my mouth.

"Are you laughing at me?"

"No. I—" I can't stop. The scene keeps playing in my mind on repeat.

The door to Smash Point swings open, and one of the staff members runs out, covering his head with his bag. He doesn't even notice us.

It's enough of a distraction, I'm finally able to string words into a normal sentence. "Was it fun?"

He considers this. Then nods his head once and says, "I think so."

The streetlight bathes us both in a dreary glow through the gray. With the deep shadows it's casting, Calder looks a little like an actor in a Halloween corn maze. I can only imagine what my face looks like now that I'm doing what Sam always calls my "kid on a roller-coaster" smile.

"What?"

I laugh. "I totally win."

"Win what."

I grab his hand and pull him out onto the non-flooded asphalt. "At life!"

"Because that's a competition?"

I adjust my shirt as best I can, but it just suctions back to my skin. "I know you don't like me. Or I'm annoying to you or something, and I get that I sometimes come across as naive—"

"When did I say I don't like you?"

I gesture to his face. "You didn't have to say it. But it's fine, I get it. I'd probably be annoyed by me, too, but I think you could use a little more of me in your life."

Calder's lips part. A drop of rain slips over his Cupid's bow and into his mouth.

I shiver and swallow hard. "I mean my personality. Since you're helping me—and we both know I'm getting the better deal here with the lessons and tips with Garrett —I just thought I could help you." This was good. I didn't want things to be awkward the next couple of weeks. Plus, if we were friends, there was less likelihood of him spilling all of this to the G-man himself.

"By making me jump in contaminated water?"

I reach out and boop his nose. "By making you have more fun." I spin and retrieve my bag from the pavement.

"Sam's right. You're a bad influence."

I grin, swiping the hair from my face. "Watch out. With that attitude, you just might end up being my best friend."

ten

MY CURSOR BLINKS on a half-written email but my brain isn't functioning, so I stack my folders for the GoodBarrel account into neat piles.

Since the company pickleball night, Garrett's been friendly. Not *flirty* friendly, but slightly more interested. Since we're moving from barely above a zero on the spectrum, it has to be at least three hundred percent growth. We talked about how the foam-core signage came in late from a vendor, and he laughed—full-body laughed—when I commented that the delivery driver's eyes reminded me of Bluecifer, the demonic blue bronco statue greeting travelers at DIA.

That tiny crack in the armor, along with Calder's advice, gave me hope. I'd pondered on my options since the night before. I needed to make Garrett believe I was interested in someone else, but he wasn't sitting over there checking off my mannerisms on a notepad (as far as I knew). He wouldn't notice if I was running my fingers through my hair or pinching the bridge of my nose, so I'd kind of need to smack him in the face with it.

But bringing up a random guy wouldn't feel natural in our current small-but-growing relationship. However . . . I could bring up a guy he knew. A guy who'd been at our pickleball night. A guy I met and knew he was friends with.

Calder wouldn't mind, would he? He was the one who gave me the advice.

I grab a file from my desk and march toward his door before I can overthink it.

When I knock, his voice filters through, warm and easy. "Come in."

He's behind his desk, sleeves rolled up. It's polka dots today, and he's already had one family call. Maybe not the best timing, but if I don't act now, I'm going to lose my nerve.

I hold up the file like a shield. "Hey, Garrett! Quick question about the Harvest Gala client mockup. I wanted to make sure you were good with the seniority order on the programs before I send to production."

He looks up, his smile flickering to life. "Yeah, sure. Let's see."

I step closer, flip open the file. He reads the first three lines, double-checking the titles. "Yep. Everything looks correct to me."

I wait for a verbal pat on the head, but when it doesn't come, I close the folder and step back. "Perfect. Thanks." He nods and is about to round the desk when I say, "So your friend who came to pickleball the other night, how do you know each other?"

His brows lift. "Calder? Uh, through pickleball actually. Why?"

"Oh, he just mentioned he's an instructor. I was thinking I'd start some lessons. Try to get past this beginner stage."

Garrett leans back in his chair with a look of shock. "You're a beginner?"

I scoff. "Yes, but thanks for that."

"I'm serious, you don't seem like a beginner."

I resist the urge to flip my hair.

Garrett picks up a pen, flipping it between his fingers. "I don't think Calder's cheap."

"Hm. Bummer. If only I got paid more at my job."

Garrett laughs. "Wow. Low blow."

"I mean, you're the one who assumed I was poor."

An amused half smile tugs at his mouth. "Let's just say, I'm not sure he'd be the best teacher."

"Oh yeah?" Was that a hint of jealousy I was picking up on?

"He knows his stuff, but he's not the most encouraging."

Something flares inside me at that comment, but I tamp it down. Garrett wasn't saying anything that wasn't true. So why did it suddenly feel like I needed to defend Calder's honor?

I cock my head to the side. "You think I need encouragement?"

Garrett's expression shifts. His chin lifts, his eyes sharpen. "I could drill with you. If you want."

"I don't know if I could afford that."

He smirks and lifts his hand. For a moment, I think he's going to run it through his hair. He doesn't. Instead, he reaches for his phone and swipes. "Monday. After work. I was planning to play at seven, but we could drill at six if you want."

I pretend to check my calendar even though anything I find that conflicts with six o'clock on Monday is instantly getting deleted. "I think that should work. Thanks."

"Of course."

I force myself to walk slowly out of the office even though I feel like I just hit a star in Mario Kart. Garrett can see through the glass into my space. I have to pretend nothing of any importance just happened for the next *five hours* even though my entire world tilted on its axis.

Garrett invited me to drill. Alone with him.

I sit at my desk and look very seriously at my computer for a few seconds before frowning a little and pulling out my phone. If he was tracking my body language, Garrett would see "concerned client communications" and nothing else. I text Sam.

> Calder's advice worked!!! Booked for a drill sesh with Garrett on Monday.

SAM

> Wow. That was fast. He didn't even have to buy you dinner first.

> Lol.

> Tell me everything

So I do. I explain my brilliant plan to use Calder as bait, and I'm halfway through my explanation of Garrett's pen twiddling when a text comes through from an unknown number.

I spot the word "lesson" and tap it open.

Hey. For lesson Thursday, can we start fifteen minutes earlier? I cleared the court time. I have to leave early for an event.
Calder

I barely take in the details because a pit opens up in my stomach. I told Garrett I was considering lessons, not that I was already taking them. What if he found out I was there? What if Megan showed up at Smash Point, saw me and Calder and Sam, and mentioned it to Garrett? It wasn't that far out of the realm of possibilities.

Hey! Actually, I think we may have to cancel Thursday anyway. A lot going on over here. Let's pick up next week.

I can't help it. I have to say something.

And your advice was excellent btw

The three dots appear. A few seconds later, Calder's message comes through.

Paddle up?

.   .   .

I laugh.

No. Competition

I didn't want to text more than that. No digital incrimination if Garrett ever found this thread.

The dots appear, then disappear. They appear again, then finally a message comes through.

Glad I could help

eleven

I SPEND the last thirty minutes of Friday afternoon updating a brand calendar, but it's almost impossible to focus. Pickleball night is upon us, and all my emotions are cranked up to full throttle. Nerves over how I'll play or what might happen with Garrett. Excitement, of course, but there's something else hiding away beneath all of that jittery energy. I can't quite put my finger on it.

I duck into the office restroom with my tote, swap my pencil skirt for the skort that has now become a wardrobe staple, and meet Sam and the others in the lobby.

Everyone's in a good mood as we walk over to The Court Collective together. The leaves are in full autumn color, dropping and swirling in the street, adding social proof to the pumpkin spice signs on display in the café window we pass.

I love this time of year. The air smells different, the sun seems a little more golden. More than anything, I look forward to the permission the colder weather gives to slow down a little bit. Something that's not easy for me to do.

After warming up, I play two games partnered with

Jerome, one with Brenda, then a prepress guy who's a real banger. I learned that term while watching Calder play the other day. There's a whole new language and culture with this sport. An underground world I knew nothing about. It feels like when I discovered poutine exists. My world is forever changed, and I'm not sure I can live without it.

I win some, lose some, remember to call the score half the time, and the whole evening runs as it should've the first time. No stress because of unexpected visitors.

I play with Garrett twice. Catch him watching me at least once. All in all a perfect night thus far.

Sam finds me between games. "You okay?"

"Yeah. Why?" I take a swig from my water bottle.

She shrugs. "I don't know. You look a little bored."

My face pinches. "What? I'm having a blast."

Her lips purse. "Okay."

"Okay?"

"Yeah. Okay." She walks toward her next court. "Just haven't heard you laughing as much."

"As much as what?" It was a Friday. I was a little worn down from the week. Sure, my energy wasn't at a ten, but what did she expect?

"I don't know. Lessons?"

My eyes widen, and I scan for Garrett. He's still in the middle of his game, which is lucky. Sam gets to keep her life tonight.

Playing pickleball here versus playing in lessons wasn't a fair comparison. In lessons, I have Calder constantly pushing my buttons. Forcing me out of my comfort zone. Here, I can just do what I'm supposed to do. Take the shots I know I've got. That's what makes a good partner, right?

It's nice to just play and let Garrett or Jerome or whoever my partner is take the tough shots. To know I don't have to do anything special, just not screw it up. When we wrap, Garrett tells me I've leveled up since last week, and I glow for an hour. That was a real compliment.

* * *

The next day is Oktoberfest with Sam, which means we commit to pretzels as a food group and joyride a pedal cart with too many seats and a custom countertop down a closed-off block with a dozen strangers who become our best friends for exactly seventy minutes. The guide has thighs like a Greek statue and a whistle he uses with far too much exuberance. The playlist is all 2000s bangers intermixed with party polkas. We cycle past a guy in lederhosen playing the accordion, which really solidifies the vibes.

Sam insists on us taking turns as "steering captain." A total farce because the wheel is fake and we all know it. But why is it so damn fun to pretend?

I have two steins of something with a name that sounds appropriately German and a third drink that smells and tastes like sour apple suckers. It's delicious and mostly sugar syrup. It makes me think of Calder, which is annoying and a little bit hot now that I'm tipsy.

"I think Calder would be fun as, like, a one-night stand."

Sam laughs. "Oh yeah?"

"Yeah. He's got that intensity, you know? I bet he's . . . really focused."

She chortles. "And Garrett's the long-term option?"

"Yeah. He's got a stable job—"

"You don't know Calder doesn't have a stable job."

I scoff. "How could he? He's always at Smash Point. Like, what does he even do besides pickleball? That's probably why he doesn't talk about himself. He doesn't want people to know he's got nothing going for him."

Sam takes a long draw from her beer, then sets it down and starts singing along to Death Cab for Cutie.

"What, no comment?"

"I have plenty of comments. I just don't think you want to hear them."

I fold my arms over the countertop and stop pedaling. "I always want to hear your comments."

Sam sets her drink in the cup holder and leans in, cupping her hand around my ear. "I think you have a thing for Calder."

"What?" I rear back, losing my balance on the bucket seat. "No! He's—no! For sure he's hot, but then you get to know him—"

"See? That's why I didn't say it."

I roll my eyes. "He's just annoying. And wildly unhappy."

"He makes you laugh."

"Because he's ridiculous." I don't have time for a stronger rebuttal because we're stopping for schnitzel and if I don't eat some solid food, I'm going to yarf.

At one stop, the barman slaps down free shots "for the pedal cart athletes," and I learn I am not, in fact, an athlete when it comes to cinnamon liquor. Sam leans her head on my shoulder on the way back, cheeks pink, eyes bright, and I think this is what makes everything in life possible.

"Maybe we should just get married," Sam says.

I laugh. "If only I loved boobs, this would all be so easy."

She swoops her hair over her shoulder, her speech slow and dreamy. "I know. But you can't ever leave, okay? You have to stay here."

Tears prick my eyes. She doesn't have to say it, I know

exactly where that's coming from. No amount of therapy can fully erase our deepest, darkest fears. We just have to learn to live with them. But it's a lot easier said than done when those fears have become a reality. Losing a friend isn't a theoretical to her.

"I'm not going anywhere, babe." I pat her cheek. We ride the rest of the way back to our meeting point humming along to "Mr. Brightside" and share a car home. She makes me get dropped off first even though I hate wondering if she's going to be okay alone in the rideshare. I know why she does that, too.

Sunday is a hangover that goes through the stages of grief. Denial (I just need to sleep a little longer), anger (who even invented light!), bargaining (if I drink two liters of water will the maracas in my brain stop?), depression (I'll never feel normal, why do I do this to myself?), and finally acceptance.

I peel myself off the couch in the afternoon, wobble to the kitchen, and put together my healing ritual of eggs, ibuprofen, and an orange. I stretch my legs, roll out my calves on a water bottle, and text with Sam.

Twice I consider asking her more about Calder's comments. But I know if I do, it's going to seem like she hit a nerve, which she absolutely didn't. The only reason I can't stop thinking about it is because it doesn't make any sense. And that he showed up in a very inappropriate dream last night. Only because we were talking about it, obviously.

All of which I need to scrub from my imagination since I have a date with Garrett tomorrow night. And I'd really like to look at the benches at the pickleball club again without my cheeks flushing.

* * *

By five on Monday my inbox is a firework show of small emergencies, but I shut the laptop and head to the restroom with my bag. I've got a new slate-blue skirt I ordered online, a white tank, and a zip-up hoodie for the walk. I pull my auburn hair into a high ponytail, secure it with a cute scrunchie, and give myself a once-over in the mirror. Low-key. Classic.

Garrett waits for me in the lobby. His eyes trail over me —he's never done that before—and he smiles. "You parked on the street?"

I nod, my cheeks heating. Was this it? Was Garrett actually interested in me? Had Calder's advice been the only missing piece I needed?

A voice that sounds a lot like Sam rings in my head. *Red flags, A.*

I slap it away. It wasn't necessarily a red flag that Garrett needed a fire under him to make an effort. That's how most guys are these days.

Garrett holds up his keys. "I got a court at a different club tonight. It had more availability. We could drive together in my car, but I was thinking I'd play at the open play after for a bit. You can stay for that, too, if you want—"

"No, that's fine. I can follow you." A new place? My heart starts to race like it knows something I don't. *It's just a different club.* "Open play sounds fun, though."

I don't want to poo-poo it, but if all the players are at Garrett's level, that would be zero percent fun for me. I'll have to watch the warm-ups before I make a decision on that.

Garrett heads for the revolving door. I trail after him, dread settling in like a weighted blanket. It couldn't be . . . could it? There were so many pickleball clubs in the city. The chances were slim. *But why didn't I just ask the name?*

"Do you want to send me the directions? In case I lose you?" Perfect. That was nonchalant.

He looks over his shoulder. "I'm a great leader."

I smile like that's exactly the answer I was hoping for, then get in my car and wait for him to pull out in front of me. We start out in the coppery light of early evening, and for ten minutes I play faithful convoy. Until he takes a left and heads west, crossing over I-25. And then turns right at the grocery store.

Noooo! He's heading straight to Smash Point, and there's nothing I can do to stop him.

twelve

GOING to Smash Point makes sense, doesn't it? If Garrett played with Calder last summer, that's probably where they met. But it's in the opposite direction from his apartment. Why wouldn't he find a place closer to him?

My hands sweat against the steering wheel. I've never scheduled lessons with Calder on Mondays. He probably isn't even going to be there, and if there's anyone else I know, I'll just play it off. Pretend we met playing somewhere else. I don't know anybody well, and Garrett did say the place had a lot of availability tonight.

I talk myself down. It's fine. There's no reason to freak out. I should never have come up with this stupid plan and should've straight up told Garrett I took a lesson with Calder and I'm a complete idiot, but it's fine.

You say that a lot. Calder's voice rings in my head. *Well, maybe that's because I'm an idiot a lot!*

Now I'm mentally arguing with him. Fantastic.

I park next to Garrett. We walk in together, laughing about a vendor snafu because that's a safe topic, but as soon as the cool air hits my face, I feel like someone hooked me up to a caffeine IV.

My eyes dart to the desk, and I breathe a silent sigh of relief. It's is manned by a guy I've never seen. Mid-twenties. Smash Point hat.

"Hey! Welcome in. First time?" he asks, looking at Garrett.

"Not for me. But I'm bringing a friend." Garrett turns to me. "I think you'll need a waiver?"

My heart lodges itself in my spine. "Oh, actually, I've played here before. It should still be on file."

"Oh, cool." Garrett looks surprised.

"Name?" the desk guy asks.

"Alecia Monroe," I say. "And could I use the Carbon demo paddle?" That was one benefit of coming here. See? Silver linings.

He nods and taps the keyboard. "Yep, you're good, your membership's still active, and—" Before I can process that, he ducks under the counter, emerges with a small branded box, and plops it on the desk like a magician revealing the rabbit. "Also, there's a note on your file. These are for you."

I blink at the box. I have a membership here? I've never paid for a membership. Did I give them my card for incidentals or something? "What are they?"

He smiles. "Open it and find out."

Garrett nudges it toward me, and I flip open the top. I pull out a zippered case, and inside is—

Garrett whistles. "Those are nice. Wow, I've seen the ads." He plucks them from the case. They look like sunglasses. "Amber lenses, vented frame. So lightweight." The logo on the temple is a green dill pickle, which I adore. "They just released this lens tint. These are amazing for tracking spin under LED lights."

"They look cool," I manage, frantically searching my brain for a reasonable explanation for this. Had Natasha or any of her friends been wearing glasses like these? Did Sam buy us both pairs? Maybe she ordered them through Smash Point?

"You two are good to go. Court four." The employee smiles, handing me my paddle.

Garrett passes the glasses back, and I place them in the case. I need to check my bank records ASAP. I consider making a break for the bathroom, but force myself to walk with Garrett to the court.

No. I will not spiral and waste any time on this tonight. The banks are already closed for the day, so whether I check it now or in three hours, it won't make a difference.

"So who do you know who plays here?" Garrett asks.

"Oh, nobody really. Just a couple of friends. Sam." I was digging myself deeper and deeper, but I couldn't seem to figure out a graceful exit.

"Well, obviously someone here is a fan." He nods to the glasses case.

I laugh. "Probably just concerned for my safety. I get hit a lot."

Garrett hangs his bag on the fence. "Yeah, how's your leg by the way?"

My breath catches. He remembers that? "Totally fine. Only lasted a few days." A week. But only because my skin is so sensitive.

I decide to put on the glasses because it would be weird if I didn't. We warm up at the net, then move on to some of his favorite drills.

"So the key is to keep your paddle up," he says for the fourth time. He shows me his grip again, even though I swear it's exactly what I'm doing. "The angle is key. You want to cheat backhand . . ."

He keeps talking. Explaining the pros and cons of different paddle positions. I listen, but my muscles are getting cold just standing here.

" . . . which will give you a huge advantage. Most women are timid up here. If you can just think about it like you're hunting. You're always looking for . . . "

I start to zone out. I remind myself that this is Garrett. This is the thing I wanted—his attention on me, and it is fully on me. I smile and nod, and when we finally start hitting again, I feel like a cyborg. The glasses are incredible. They completely cut the glare from the overhead lights, and I swear it's easier for me to track the ball. That, combined with my muscle memory finally clicking, equals me hitting beautiful drives from the baseline.

Garrett grins and takes full credit even though it has nothing to do with a word he said. I let him claim it, but it itches under my skin a little.

"Hey, that's so much better!" Garrett is lit up like a Christmas tree as we break for water. It doesn't feel like he's complimenting me, more his own coaching abilities.

"Thank you." I grab my water bottle and take a drink. "I think I'll refill this really quick."

"Yeah, good idea."

We walk to the water fountain between the restrooms and top off our bottles. Mine doesn't take much, but Garrett's is almost empty.

I lecture myself while I wait. Why am I being such a downer tonight? I'm here with Garrett! I should be getting to know him better or flirting or something other than allowing my eyes to wander to other courts, worrying about what exactly?

There's nobody I know here. We have a half an hour left on our court, and then I can play a few games if I want, otherwise I can go home. *Just lock the heck in, Alecia.*

"There we go." Garrett turns and screws on the lid.

The front doors open as we walk past the registration desk, and the air shifts. I look up automatically and freeze. Calder walks in wearing his navy-blue staff tee and gray shorts, his hat on backward. He turns his head and stops, his eyes locking on the glasses I'm wearing, and I instantly know.

They're from him. Calder got me the glasses. My stomach feels like it's being scooped out like a pumpkin. Why would he do something like that?

I'm not a nice guy.

His attention flicks to Garrett standing next to me. A muscle in his jaw ticks. "Hey. What are you doing here?"

thirteen

THE QUESTION ISN'T for Garrett, it's for me. After that one look in Garrett's direction, Calder barely acknowledges he exists. Which is weird for someone who's supposed to be a friend.

Calder got me these glasses. Did he also get me the membership? Was that part of taking lessons here? A perk?

"Oh, just doing some drilling after work," Garrett answers.

I wince as Calder's eyebrow quirks.

"Huh."

Garrett strides forward and claps him on the shoulder. "Glad to see you, buddy. I wasn't sure you'd make it tonight."

My eyes narrow. *Garrett knew Calder was coming?*

The doors open again to more players, and realization dawns. Right. Open play. Everyone's going to be showing up in the next thirty minutes.

Garrett walks back to me. "Want to get some mini games in before open play?"

I nod. Calder rounds the desk and busies himself with

something in his bag as I start back toward our court. I need to explain this. Tell him Garrett had no idea we'd done lessons already. Calder would understand. He was the one who gave me the idea in the first place.

Garrett waits by the gate, and his hand lands on my lower back as I walk through. I stiffen. Has he ever touched me like that before? I glance up, but see his head turned toward the desk where Calder is still standing.

Our court is closest to the front desk.

Garrett knew Calder was coming.

"Is that a new skirt?" Garrett's hand shifts to my hip, as he cocks his head to look at me.

"Yeah."

"I like the color."

The words feel oily, and pull back, pretending I'm in a hurry to get on the other side of the net. So. Garrett had planned this. Did he actually want to spend time with me or was our so-called date just a pissing match?

Garrett suggests we play skinny court. Similar to seven-eleven but we both start at the baseline and work our way up to the net. He serves, and I smack the ball back deep. These are the shots I'm most comfortable with.

Garrett hits a drop, and I'm already in the mid-court. I drive it. I know the goal is to drop it, but I don't have it in me. I need to hit something. Hard.

Garrett blocks, but he obviously wasn't ready for that shot. "Wow," he laughs. "That break got you fired up."

"You could say that."

He tosses me the ball, and I serve it. When I drive his return, he's ready for it. Something in his face changes—interest? Challenge? He starts taking it seriously now, matching my pace. The ball speeds up between us.

He laughs again. "Where's this been hiding?"

I grin tightly and snap another shot toward him.

It's stupid because he can easily hit these back. He sends the ball to my feet, and I miss my next shot into the net.

Garrett's breathing heavy. "You're a little scary."

I can't tell if that's a compliment or another performance. My skin feels too hot, my hands jittery. It's only made worse by the fact that our audience is growing. We play a few more points, then I tell Garrett I should probably finish up.

The decision to stay for open play or not has never felt easier.

"This was fun," I say as I head for my bag.

"Yeah, we should do it again sometime."

How I'd wished to hear those words just a week ago. Now they fell a little flat. "That would be great."

"Don't leave without saying goodbye."

I salute him and head to the restrooms, the noise of the courts fading behind me. Right before I push through the door, movement catches my eye, and I look right instead of left. Calder's at an open locker.

There's no thinking before my next move. I rush forward, grab his arm, and pull him into one of the open shower rooms and close the door. "You can't tell him we already had lessons."

"Who, Garrett?"

I nod. "Yes, Garrett. Who else?"

Calder's eyes narrow. "Why not?"

"Because. You said he needed competition, so I asked about you! I pretended I was interested in lessons. Like—" I press my fingers to my temples. "Like I was interested in you."

His eyebrows lift. "You asked Garrett about me?"

"Yes! It was the only thing that made sense. You've seen the guys at work."

"What about Jerome?"

I smack his chest. "Shut up."

The corner of his mouth turns up, and I'm suddenly very aware of how close we're standing.

Calder blows out a breath. "Lies. The perfect start to a budding relationship."

"Oh come on! Everyone lies a little at the beginning of a relationship."

He crosses his arms, and they nearly brush my chest. "I don't."

"Really. You've never told a white lie to get to know someone?"

He considers that. "No."

"Well. Add me to your prayer list so I can ride your coattails to heaven." I try to push past him to get to the door, but he doesn't move. "I need to go."

"Was Garrett good at drilling?"

I groan. "Oh my gosh, you're the worst."

"Did he have gentle hands?"

I laugh in spite of myself, then tip my chin up to level my eyes at him. "I drove hard. He took it like a man." Not exactly the metaphor I was going for, but the look on Calder's face is worth it.

A flush crawls up his neck. "Surprising. Garrett's the kind of guy who likes control."

"Hm. Garrett had plenty to say about you, too."

I regret saying that instantly. Calder's face clouds over, his eyes like an arctic lake. The air thickens, my skin buzzing. Calder shifts on his feet, and for a half second, I expect him to lean in. To put his hand out. To—

He steps back, leaving the door in plain view. "Staying for open play?"

I swallow, my throat thick. "No."

He drops his eyes, nodding. "Well. I won't break your cover."

I fight to catch my breath without making it obvious I'm about to pass out. "Great. Thanks." My hand somehow finds the handle. I drop it and yank, sucking in air as soon as I clear the threshold.

* * *

The market on Tuesday afternoon sprawls down 16th Street like a painter spilled a palette of color. White tents billow in the breeze, and the smell of roasted nuts mingles with fresh espresso and something herbal—lavender, maybe? The afternoon sun glints off the glass towers behind the booths, and the whole street hums with music and chatter. If anyone at Paper and Pixel wants to take the client gift purchasing assignment from me, they'll have to pry it from my cold, dead hands.

I wander between vendors with my phone balanced on my shoulder, Sam's voice in my ear. I forgot my earbuds back at the office. "So, let me get this straight—you *dragged* him into the shower room?"

"I *pulled* him," I correct, scanning a display of hand-thrown mugs shaped like mountain peaks. "There was no dragging."

"Semantics. You locked yourself in with him."

"I didn't *lock* it," I protest. "And I didn't plan it. It was just heat of the moment. I needed him to not say anything to Garrett."

"Uh-huh."

I finger a mug painted in a wash of turquoise and gold, pretending I'm not thinking about Calder's face when I mentioned Garrett talking about him. "He said he wouldn't rat me out."

"Well, yeah. Of course he won't."

I frown. "What does that mean?"

Sam exhales. "You know what it means, babe. We already talked about this."

"Girl. He's not into me, and I'm . . . I don't know what I am." That was the truth. Confused. Probably the best adjective at the moment.

I choose a couple of mugs and some gourmet hot chocolate, then hand my card to the vendor. "He gave me pickleball glasses."

"Garrett?" she hisses.

"No. Calder."

The woman wraps the mugs carefully, tucking them into a stamped recycled-paper bag.

"You didn't want to tell me."

"Right."

"Because it's evidence that improves my theory."

"Maybe." I take the bag and weave through the crowd toward a table stacked with candles that smell like the inside of a fruit bowl. "He said he never tells white lies. Like when he's interested in someone."

She laughs. "Well, la-dee-da."

"That's what I said!"

The air fills with the echo of a busker's guitar, and I pause to listen a moment.

Sam perks up. "Hey, Megan was telling me there's a singles' night at Smash Point tomorrow night. Want to go?"

"Middle of the week?"

"Apparently they switch it up. It starts at six thirty. They've got food and drinks."

My phone beeps with another call. "Yeah, sure. I'll go with you." I pull the phone down to look at the screen and almost choke. Garrett. His number's been in my phone since I got the job, but I don't think he's used it once.

"Sam. It's Garrett."

"What?"

"He's calling! I'm going to go, I'll call you—"

"Go! Go."

I hang up and switch to the next call, almost forgetting to breathe. "Hey, Garrett."

"Hey. I heard you're out shopping."

I laugh. "Yep, it's the best job."

"Sorry to bug you, I know it's late in the day."

"No worries," I say, stepping aside to let a woman with a stroller pass. "What's up?"

"I, uh…" He chuckles. "This is really last-minute, but I have to go to this dinner tonight. Client event thing, kind of schmoozy. I just found out they're expecting me to bring a plus-one."

I blink. "Oh?"

"Yeah." He pauses. "I thought since you'll likely be working on this project, you'd be an obvious fit. Plus, I had a great time last night."

I expect that to send my heart fluttering, but it stays stone quiet. Odd.

"Would you be interested in coming with me?"

My phone buzzes against my cheek. I look at the screen and see a text from Sam.

He's in the breakroom. Running his HANDS through his HAIR.

For a heartbeat, I forget how to hold my phone. "Tonight?" I echo, a little breathless.

"Yeah, sorry. Totally fine if you can't."

"No, I—"

Garrett is talking to me, asking me out. He's checking all the boxes for *me*.

"You still there?" he asks, voice a little uncertain.

"Yeah," I say quickly. "Sorry, someone bumped me. So, the dinner, I think that should work. What time?"

"Six thirty. At Barolo Grill."

I blink again. *Barolo Grill.* One of the fanciest Italian restaurants in the city. "That sounds amazing."

"Great." Relief filters through his voice, and it's so genuine that it steadies me. "Why don't you head home when you're done? No need to come back to the office. I'll pick you up at six?"

"Six works. I'll see you then."

fourteen

GARRETT'S TEXT comes at 5:59.

I'm still pacing in front of my living room mirror, adjusting my earrings for the sixth time. My closet wasn't built for a fancy client dinner. It's built for work chic and impulse farmer's market rendezvous. Mostly just lounging after work. In my robe.

In the end, I went with my emergency date outfit—soft navy wrap dress, gold hoops, hair down in a wave that only half obeyed my curling iron. I throw on nude heels and grab a beige clutch. Hopefully classic and approachable.

When I step outside, Garrett's silver car is idling at the curb, sleek and polished. He gets out as I approach and rounds the car to open my door. A perfect gentleman. "You look great."

"Thanks," I say, trying not to trip on the curb as I slide into the passenger seat.

His car smells like cedarwood and leather. He adjusts the temperature down a degree, then glances at me with a grin. "Thanks again for coming last-minute. These client things are always more fun with someone else there. And you're good with people."

The compliments are kind of freaking me out, if I'm being honest. Especially after last night. I have no idea if he means them or if he's just saying the right thing at the right moment.

"That's one way to put it." I fasten my seatbelt. "I'm good at talking a lot."

He pulls away from the curb. "Just ask questions. People love talking about themselves."

I let out a puff of air. *Some* people loved talking about themselves. "Did you have fun at open play?"

Garrett nods. "Yeah, it's always a good time."

"You play there a lot?"

He shakes his head. "Not since I moved."

Ah. So that's why he had a connection to Smash Point. He used to live closer. "Do you and Calder still play tournaments together?"

"No. I'd be open to it though. He's still got the shots of a pro even if his shoulder's not quite back yet."

Blood rushes in my ears. "Oh, he used to be pro?"

Garrett nods. "Yeah, he was on the PPA circuit. Had a few sponsorships. I didn't know him back then, but I've watched his clips."

I mentally kick myself. First rule of meeting new people: Google them. How had I missed that? My fingers fidget over the edges of my phone in my clutch.

Outside the window, Denver glows in the amber dusk. Garrett starts talking about a new client, an eco-friendly packaging company that could be a huge account for us. He outlines their sustainability goals, their brand philosophy, their leadership team. I nod at the right times, occasionally tossing in a "That's smart" or "Oh, I love that."

Internally, I'm doing a whole different calculus. About my posture and where to put my hands. I want to sound sharp but warm, curious but not overeager. All while wishing I could press pause on the night, slide into the back seat, and look up videos of Calder.

"So, this is kind of a big deal for them?" I ask as we hit a red light.

"Yeah. They just expanded into national retail chains. The dinner's their way of celebrating, and making sure we're still the right partner as they scale."

"So, no pressure."

He smiles, reaching across the console to squeeze my hand. "You'll be perfect." He doesn't let go, and something that's been niggling at me all evening works its way to the surface.

"I'm honestly surprised you didn't ask Megan. She seems perfect for this kind of thing." It was true. If I wanted to impress a client, as much as I love myself, she'd be the obvious choice.

His hand twitches. "Megan's great, but she's got her own priorities."

"Oh?"

"No, I just mean she doesn't work on the client side. When she leaves the office, she's checked out."

I frown. "But she organized the pickleball night. Seems like she's open to some extracurriculars." I don't know why

I'm arguing with him, but something about what he said rubs me the wrong way.

"For sure. Just the ones she's interested in." He pulls his hand back and adjusts the temperature again, then clears his throat. "You're the obvious choice, by the way. Don't sell yourself short."

I smile, but something twists in my gut, just like it did the night before. I'm grateful when he starts asking questions about the market. He's using his own conversational tactic, and I'm glad to play into it. Candles and mugs don't make me feel queasy.

We pull up to Barolo Grill ten minutes later, and the valet lane gleams under the string lights. Garrett hands off the keys and places a steady hand at the small of my back as we walk through the doors.

Inside, everything smells like garlic and rosemary, the faint hum of a jazz trio drifting from the bar. The host greets Garrett by name and leads us to a private dining room off the main floor. Gold-toned light pools over a long table draped in linen, dotted with wine glasses and neatly folded menus.

Most of the seats are already filled. Garrett's smile switches effortlessly to work mode as he introduces me around. "This is Alecia Monroe, she's one of our marketing leads and an absolute lifesaver."

The introductions blur into a parade of first names, handshakes, and smiles. I laugh at the right moments, sip my wine, and manage to remember at least half of their names. Lillian, the client's co-founder, is warm and sharp. Her husband, quieter, tells me about their new packaging plant in Golden.

I let Garrett do most of the talking at first. He's good at it. Just the right amount of charm, the perfect anecdotes. I chime in when needed, agreeing and adding a note of humor here and there. The perfect partner.

Everything is going smoothly. But by the time the main course arrives, Lillian and I get talking about women's clothing trends, and I forget that I'm supposed to be smooth and polished, asking questions instead of taking over.

It takes all of two minutes for my non-work personality to come out in a big way. "It's always the waistbands. In underwear, especially. Just accept that we have love handles and make them thicker! Or stretchier. There are really a thousand options that aren't floss used to cut cakes."

The woman next to us nearly chokes on her wine laughing. Lillian wipes tears from her eyes.

Garrett's hand brushes my knee under the table. When I glance at him, he's smiling, but he gives me a look.

I read it perfectly because it's the exact look I used to get from my mom growing up. *That's a little much. Pull back a bit. Be a little less of you.*

I don't expect it to hit me so hard, but it does. At a certain point, all the little hits add up, and the breath gets knocked right out of you.

I pluck my napkin off my lap. "Excuse me. I'll be right back." I mouth "Bathroom" to Garrett when he looks apologetic, then escape before he can read the hurt on my face.

The women's restroom is dim and elegant, all marble counters and golden sconces. I lock myself in a stall and lean against the door as I pull out my phone.

I flip to my messages with Sam.

You up? I need to rant.

I wait, but the three dots don't appear. The muffled laughter from the dining room seeps through the walls. This isn't how it's supposed to feel, is it? Garrett asked me here, but it feels like *me* is the last thing he wants. He wants the version of me that makes him look good. That fits the company brand style guide.

I scroll through my texts again, thumb hovering over Sam's name, willing her to text back.

Nothing.

Then I remember how much I wanted my phone earlier and flip to my browser. I type in Calder's name from his email. Pickleball clips immediately populate my results, and I click on the first one. *Almost a million views?*

I'm entranced. His back is to me in the clip, but I would know it was him anywhere just by the way he moves. Smooth and focused. I watch to the end and am about to start another when I realize numbing out to a guilty pleasure isn't going to solve my current problem.

I go back to my texts and my thumb flicks down, scrolling instinctively, and lands on another name. I snort. When did I add Calder as a contact? And why did I put his name in like that? Probably another casualty of Oktoberfest.

I hesitate over our last conversation. My rational brain says this is definitely not a good idea. But my sad and frustrated brain that is about to go out there and eat a metric ton of pasta says it's imperative.

> Hey. Theoretically. What would you do if you were stuck at a work dinner and forgot how to be normal?

My heart races. I'm about to unsend it when the dots appear. *Frederick Calder the Third is typing.*

ALECIA

> Hey. Theoretically. What would you do if you were stuck at a work dinner and forgot how to be normal?

CALDER

> Define normal

> You know. Professional. Charming. The kind of person who doesn't make underwear jokes in front of clients

> Sounds like the best part of the dinner

> Not according to Garrett

Garrett's there?

He is, in fact

What else did he say about me?

Typical Frederick. Only concerned about himself. I'm in a crisis here, remember?

Right. Send the debrief later

I would say normal is overrated

The data I've collected doesn't skew that direction

What kind of data?

Dating data

Don't pretend you have numbers. Just say it's how you feel

That's the most compelling data

CALDER

So because you're single, you think there's something wrong with you

ALECIA

That is the very conclusion. Yes.

And this work dinner . . .

Garrett asked me to come

So it's a date

Kind of

And if you're normal he'll what? Ask you on another one?

That's the hope

Where are you?

Why does that matter?

I'm imagining you ignoring Garrett at the table. Which I love, by the way

Bathroom. Surprised you're not here.

Wow

It's kind of our thing

Done with another ice pack? I could throw it away for you

OMG

FOCUS

Right. You want to go on another date with Garrett so you can hide in the bathroom

The ambiance is unreal. Tampon dispenser 10/10

Can't wait to see the wedding invitations.
Garrett and the shell of Alecia invite you to
share their special day

Stop! I can't breathe!

How do you recommend this works? I
annoy you, too

You make me uncomfortable.

And that's different how?

Very different

Opposite actually

Does annoyed have an opposite?

CALDER

I don't think I've met anyone like you

ALECIA

Ugh. See? That's the problem though.
People like what they're used to

They like safe bets. No risk, no reward

That's a nice thing to say, Frederick

Not a nice guy, remember, Mabel?

You said you never lie

If it were me, I'd suffer through dinner. Then head over to Smash Point after to blow off some steam

Might not be home until past nine. Is it open that late?

For you it is

I SIT in my car for a full minute staring at the neon Smash Point Social sign while my stomach does a small trapeze act. I debated staying home after Barolo. Spending another hour at the table post text conversation with Calder used every mental muscle I had to act the way Garrett wanted me to. I was tempted to wipe off the makeup, hang up the dress, make chamomile tea, and chill.

But Calder's text was still sitting on my phone. That won out.

Now, I get out of the car, grab my bag, and walk to the door, fully expecting it to be locked, but it swings open easily. Inside, two courts are still going. A couple on court one locked in hand battles, and a young woman with someone who looks to be her coach. I smile to myself. Nothing like a late-night drill sesh.

There's nobody at the front desk to check in with, so I walk toward Calder, stretching on court two. He glances up as I step through the gate, and the way his eyes do that quick head-to-toe inventory makes my heart skip.

"Hey." He straightens, and the look on his face is pure innocence. The scowl I'm so used to seeing there is softened, his lips slightly parted, his long lashes shadowing his cheeks. It's disarming as hell.

"Hey." I lift a hand. I swapped the Barolo dress for leggings and an oversized crewneck over a tank top. We both know why I'm here. At least, I think we do? Calder has to know how flirty he was being. But as he picks up his paddle and walks toward the net, my confidence wanes. Was he just being nice?

He pulls a ball from his pocket. "How'd the rest of dinner go?"

"I was the picture of professionalism."

He huffs a breath. "Garrett was happy?"

"More than happy." I get in position opposite him.

Calder pauses, about to hit the ball. "What does that mean?"

"I think he hoped our night would've been extended." Garrett drove me home and turned off the car before I told him I had plans to do a workout. I'd thought about saying I was exhausted and needed to head to bed, but Calder's stance on white lies got to me. Why was I trying to make the truth easier to hear? Garrett wasn't going to like that I was turning him down either way, so I may as well be honest.

"Huh." Calder sends the ball over the net.

"I just—" I hit it back. "I don't get why dating has to be so hard. Why do we have to play this game with each other? Or maybe it's just with myself."

We dink back and forth, and my legs start to warm up. "Thank you, by the way."

"For what?"

My hands start to tingle. "For your text messages."

Calder nods once, but when he doesn't comment, I can't leave it alone. "I don't know how I feel about everything, though. Like, I'm not supposed to want or need to be with someone. I'm supposed to be happy on my own, and I am, but not really, you know? Life is more fun when you do it with other people. I have friends, and don't get me wrong, they're amazing, but I want romantic love. Is that lame to admit?"

Calder's brows are pinched again. "No. Not lame." He moves back from the kitchen line, and I follow his lead, hitting deeper balls.

"But then it feels like I have to try because it's not just happening."

Calder hits a diabolical angle, and I barely get it back. "Nice," he says, and warmth blooms in my chest.

"You're right, though," I continue. "I don't want to be with someone who doesn't like who I am. Or, I guess, only likes part of who I am. But is it possible for someone to love everything?"

"Hey! Do you two want to play a game?" the woman on the court next to us calls over. She's probably in her mid-fifties, wearing a neon visor and bright pink shoes. I already love her.

Calder glances at me questioningly, and I nod.

We hop onto their court, and I'm instantly nervous. Especially knowing that Calder used to be on the pro circuit. I want to ask him about that. I want to know how he got so good—he must've played racquet sports growing up —and what it was like traveling around to tournaments. I want to know every girl he ever dated, where he went to school, and what his family is like. I want to know every-thing about him.

"Nice glasses." The woman's husband steps up to the net. "I'm Pete."

"Thanks." I give Calder a sidelong glance. "I'm Alecia."

"Julie." The woman puts out her hand and I shake it. They both already know Calder. Everyone here knows Calder.

"You want to serve first?" Pete asks, nodding at the ball in Calder's hand. "Oh wait, what ball are you using?"

I watch Calder's face with a grin. He draws a very intentional breath. "Uh, not sure." He flips the ball over. "Looks like Selkirk."

"Mind if we use this? Just love our Vulcans."

"Sure." Calder tosses the ball back onto our court.

I take the ball from Pete and turn to the baseline. "That was very big of you."

"Don't."

"I'm just saying, if I didn't know you, I wouldn't have been able to tell you wanted to punch him in the face."

Calder fights back a smile.

I pause for dramatic effect. "I'm really proud."

Calder puts his hands on his hips and gives me a look. I flash a cheesy smile and bounce the ball once before getting into serving position. "I'm sorry. Just putting that out there in advance."

Calder frowns. "Why?"

"Because of what's about to happen."

"You're better than you give yourself credit for."

I scoff. "Well, I don't play like you."

"Good partners usually don't."

Out of nowhere, the night's events tumble over me a second time. *Was that the problem?* I want Garrett because he seems a little like me? Maybe I'm thinking about things all wrong. Maybe I need someone who doesn't play like me. Who makes me think differently about the world. Who makes me a little uncomfortable.

"Ready?" Calder watches me, and I snap out of it.

"Yep." I serve, blessedly keeping the ball inside the lines.

After a few points, I decide Pete and Julie are the most fun people I've ever played with. They make good shots, but they laugh it off when they miss the ball. They tease each other and us, and don't take any of it too seriously.

When Julie notices Calder taking it easy, she calls him out. "Kill me on the angle if I'm out of position, Calder! Don't be nice!"

He laughs, and I'm instantly obsessed with the sound. With the smile lines on his face. I need to see that again. I need to see it every day.

My heart races for every reason except that I'm rushing around the court chasing a ball.

As usual, Sam knows me better than I know myself. I do, in fact, seem to have a major thing for Calder.

"You're quiet," Calder says after we tap paddles on round one.

"Am I?" I brush the comment off and jog to my water bottle on our court. I'm being weird. I know it, but I can't do anything to stop it. Now that I've acknowledged it, everything Calder does is lighting me on fire.

We play another game and a half with them before the staff member up front lets us know his cleaning is all done and he needs to shut down. Smash Point technically closed over half an hour ago, based on the lettering on the door. I love that he let us all play for extra time.

The four of us chat as we grab our things, then walk to

the parking lot together. I'm dying to talk with Calder alone, but can't figure out how to make it happen.

The parking lot looks like a spill of ink with only four cars dotting the two halos created by the light. Julie and Pete wave goodbye and hop in their SUV.

Calder and I are parked on opposite sides.

I adjust the strap of my bag on my shoulder. "Well, thanks for this."

"Glad you could come." He looks like he's about to say something else, but doesn't.

Just as I'm about to make a joke about talking with him in the ladies' restroom again sometime, I catch a small flicker of movement in the red glow of Julie and Pete's tail-lights. A tiny brown lump—

"Stop!" I gasp, grabbing Calder's hand and running into the lot. I wave my free hand until Pete sees me and brakes. He rolls down his window.

"Sorry! There's just a rabbit!" I drop my bag and run behind the vehicle, sinking to my knees on the asphalt. "Calder, can you go to the front in case it bolts?"

Pete and Julie are already out of their seats. They each take a side of the SUV between the wheels. We have every exit covered.

I reach for the baby bunny. It jolts and turns, but when it doesn't see an obvious path, it rushes next to the wheel and I'm able to scoop it up. "Got it!" It's ears are slicked back, its little heart staccatto.

"Hi," I whisper. "I'm not going to hurt you, okay?"

"You almost ran it over, Pete!" Julie brushes off her knees.

"Didn't even see the thing."

Julie sighs. "How could you? He was probably hiding under the car."

"I bet the engine scared him out," I say.

Calder motions to the field next to the parking lot, and I follow him over, leaving our bags on the pavement.

"Have a good night you two!" Julie calls, and Calder waves for both of us.

He walks up to the fence and finds a gap, lifting the chain link so I can push the bunny through. The little guy sits there for a moment, but as soon as Calder drops his hand, he takes off into the grass.

Calder bends the fence straight. It doesn't fully meet the ground, but that's not a problem we can solve tonight.

"We saved a bunny." I straighten and am about to brush the hair that escaped my elastic out of my face when Calder catches my wrists.

"Don't touch anything."

"Wha—?"

"You just touched a wild animal. We need to wash your hands."

"I have sanitizer in the car."

He shakes his head. "No way. You need to wash with soap."

I snort. "It's fine, I only held him for two seconds."

"Three minutes, and bacteria doesn't hang out before it decides to transmit to your hands."

He lets go of my arms carefully, watching to make sure I'm being obedient.

"I won't touch anything. Promise. But where can I wash my hands? Smash Point is close—"

Calder takes off. He runs to the front of the building and knocks. The employee must still be in there because the door opens.

I jog over as fast as I can with my hands still outstretched, and when I arrive, Calder motions me inside.

"Doors are locked. When you leave you won't be able to get back in," the staff member instructs.

"Got it." Calder walks with me through the entryway. The lights are all off except for two emergency lights.

I bump into something on my right and laugh. "I'm going to fall flat on my face."

"This way." Calder's hand slips around my waist, and I shiver. "Sorry."

"No, I like it. I mean, I like that you're keeping me upright." I would've face-palmed if I weren't worried Calder would then make me take a full-body shower.

He leads me into the restroom and the motion lights flick on.

"Don't touch the handle." He walks past me and turns on the warm water, then waits for me to put my hands under the soap dispenser, and pushes the button.

I rub the soap between my palms.

He grimaces. "What are you doing?"

"Washing my hands."

"You're just rubbing raw soap around?"

I laugh. "Yeah. I want to get it evenly distributed."

"You have to add some water first."

"But then the water washes off all the soap."

He looks away, horrified. Which of course only fuels my soap rubbing.

I move back into his line of sight, ignoring the rushing water in the sink. "I really love getting it in every nook and cranny, you know?"

"Gross." He turns around.

"It's like ASMR." The soap crackles and pops as I work it through my fingers.

He growls and turns back, grabbing my arms. I squeal

as he drags me to the sink, but I'm laughing too hard to put up a fight.

Calder shoves my hands under the water and threads his fingers with mine, lathering up the soap between us. "See? Water makes it work."

"It's a good thing I got it everywhere though because—"

He flips my hands and runs his thumbs over my palms, and my laughter dies. It's replaced with liquid heat shooting up my arms and dropping directly into my lady parts.

Calder runs his hands over mine until he's convinced the soap is gone, then turns off the water. He's about to reach for a paper towel, but I plant my hands directly on his chest. He looks down, the corner of his mouth lifting, then places his wet hands on me.

I suck in a breath. He's touching my boobs. He's straight-up hands on my bra, and I'm so shocked, I burst out laughing.

Calder breaks, and we stand there, busting our guts, with our hands soaking each other's shirts.

"Hey, Calder?" A voice filters through the door, and we jolt apart. "Are you—?"

The restroom door flies open. The employee we just left at the front takes us in. First our faces, then his eyes drop to the identical dark handprints on our shirts.

I purse my lips as his face shifts from surprise to confusion.

He clears his throat. "You were taking a while, so I wanted to make sure—"

"We're good." Calder says without a hint of amusement. "Just leaving."

The employee nods. "Cool. Yeah." He steps back so we

can exit, and we take the walk of shame to the front with heads held high.

"Thank you!" I say, as we rush out into the night.

I start laughing again the second the door closes behind us. "Did you see his—?"

Calder throws an arm over my shoulder and clamps his hand over my mouth. "Shh. He's right behind us."

I grab his wrist and force his hand down so I can breathe. I can't quite stop my laughter, but I do keep it quiet. Calder walks me to where Julie and Pete were parked so we can collect our bags.

He picks them both up and hands me mine.

"Thank you." I grin at him, and his eyes sparkle under the street lamp. "Your eyes are pretty."

"Thank you." Calder's face is still pulled into a smirk. We stand there a moment, studying each other, and then he says, "I think it's delighted. Or enchanted."

My face scrunches with confusion. "What?"

He wets his lips. "The opposite of annoyed."

My heart stills in my chest. Goosebumps lift in a wave over my arms and neck.

Calder drops his head, then turns to his car. "Goodnight, Alecia."

I watch him go, my feet planted in the asphalt. For the first time in my life, I'm stunned speechless.

When he's halfway to his car, I finally convince my body to move. I turn and walk to my car in a daze. I'm so worried I'm going to forget this moment that I want to drive to a tattoo shop and get those two words permanently inscribed on my body.

And why are we walking away from each other right now? Why didn't I grab him and kiss the hell out of his face? Missed opportunity and then some.

I throw my bag in the back seat of my car, then spin when I hear footsteps. I barely have time to process that it's Calder before he's pressing me up against the car, his body flush against mine, his hand tugging on my ponytail to tip my head back.

"If it's okay, I changed my mind."

<h1 style="text-align:center">seventeen</h1>

I NOD.

Calder's lips crash over mine, and I steal his breath. My hands sneak up the back of his shirt, drawing him closer. The metal of the car is cool against my back, his palm warm where it anchors me. His mouth moves like he already knows what I'll taste like. Like this isn't moving forward, but catching up.

I'm dizzy and delirious, wondering how I can pull his tall frame through the door of my car and stretch out with him in the back seat. I want him everywhere. His hands, his weight.

And then Calder pulls back. I press forward, trying to keep him there, and he grins. He presses his hands on my shoulders until I'm steady, then tucks a strand of hair behind my ear.

He clears his throat and runs his thumb over his lower lip. "Goodnight."

"Mmhmm." It's all I can manage. Again with the missed opportunities.

——

CALDER

No rabbit fever?

ALECIA

Free and clear. My soap method worked.

Good morning

Good morning. Did I tell you how you show up in my phone?

I don't think I want to know

Frederick Calder the Third

So much better than I was thinking

Are you a "third?"

Sadly not even a second

It makes sense when you think about it

Let us all hope that the genetic mental slide culminating in this naming disaster ends with me

I grin into the rim of my mug and send him a photo of the window light slanting across my desk, the way it turns my stack of paper swatches into something jewel-like. It's random and pointless, but it's pretty and I think he might like it.

I'm at my desk early for once, hair in a low ponytail since I didn't have time to wash it after all the shenanigans last night, a soft sweater over a pair of loose jeans. I work my way through my inbox, but it's slow going since I keep getting distracted.

CALDER

> You sleep okay?

ALECIA

> I can think of ways I could've slept better

> Melatonin?

> Is that what the kids call it these days?

It's ridiculous how easy it is to talk to him. How the space between text bubbles feels like oxygen instead of a candle snuffer. Sam's in a meeting this morning, and I'm dying to talk with her about last night. Lunch can't come too soon.

I'm lining up dielines when a knock raps softly at my

open door. I look up and see Garrett framed there in a crisp shirt. "Hey. Do you have a minute?"

My shoulders tense. Garrett also doesn't know what happened last night, and by the smile on his face and the box he's holding, I'm thinking it's not going to be a welcome revelation.

He steps in and sets the small black box on my desk.

"What's this?" My voice is breathy. I'm already starting to sweat.

"A thank-you," he says. "For last night. You were great."

I open the lid and it's a pen. Sleek, titanium. The clip gleams, our brand name embossed on the side.

Wow. Not at all what I was expecting. "Thank you. It's beautiful." It's very . . . Garrett.

"Figured you'd appreciate it." He tips his head toward my array of well-loved felt-tips. "Thought you could use something a bit nicer."

Something inside me shuts like a trapdoor. Was this seriously what I'd wanted? To be noticed by him?

"Garrett," I start, and then stop.

He misreads my pause as delighted awe, which is fair. Other women have surely trained him for this. He slips a hand in his pocket. "You saved me from a long night of shop talk. And you looked—" he waves a hand, searching for the right word "—fantastic."

There it is again. A compliment that lands on the surface and refuses to sink. I'm sure I did look fine, but it was a wrap dress. I looked appropriate. Garrett doesn't know the half of how fantastic I can show up.

I set the lid on the box down gently. "I should tell you something. And I want to say it before this gets weird."

His smile hitchhikes toward concern. "Okay."

"I did end up taking a lesson at Smash Point."

His brows lift. "Oh. Nice. With who?"

I purse my lips. "With Calder."

Something shifts in his expression. Small, but sharp. "You said—"

"I know." I put a hand up. "I started with a different instructor, he got injured, and that time fit my schedule. When I asked about Calder, I was . . ." I shake my head. "I don't know. Trying to get your attention."

He's quiet a beat too long. Then he nods, his smile cooling a few degrees. "Right."

"This is really kind, but I can't accept this." I nudge the box back across the desk.

He stares at it. "It's just a pen, Alecia." When I don't take it back, he exhales through his nose. Almost a laugh, but not at all amused. "Okay. So you're interested in him or something?"

"I am."

Garrett shakes his head. "You've met him, what, twice?"

My shirt from last night would insist we'd more than met. "We've talked a few times." My phone buzzes on my desk with Calder's name at the top.

Garrett slides the pen box off the wood. "Well. Give it a few more times, and I'm sure you'll figure it out." He turns to the door, but that comment sends me right back to the night before. His hand on my knee, his subtle head shake.

"Figure what out, Garrett?"

He turns back, a hint of surprise on his face. He considers his words, then shrugs. "That he's not your type. And I think he's into Sam, by the way."

I blink. *Sam?* I ignore that for the moment. "You know my type?"

"We've worked together all year, so—"

"What exactly do you know about me?" I fold my arms

over my chest. "Honestly, had you not walked in here just now, I would've said you didn't know where my office was."

Garrett gives me a look, but I'm not smiling. "You're kidding, right?"

"No. Not kidding." I round the desk and half sit on the edge. "It's hilarious because I've had a thing for you for months, and the first time you noticed me was after I mentioned another guy."

He scoffs. "That's—no, that's not—"

"Why did you say you'd drill with me? And then take me to Smash Point?"

"Because I had open play after."

"Nothing to do with Calder showing up and seeing us together?"

His jaw tightens, and he shakes his head. "I was trying to be nice."

"Have you ever asked about my life? My family? My hobbies?"

"I asked about pickleball."

"I signed up for you! I didn't even know how to play pickleball, but then I saw you were into it and there was that sign up, so I figured I could learn—"

"Wait, you'd never played before?"

I laugh. "No! That's why I signed up for lessons at Smash Point."

"Damn. Well, you fooled me."

I slump, pressing my palms into the desk. "It's pathetic, I know."

He looks down at his hands, his face coloring. "Well. I'm sorry. I didn't realize."

I groan. "It's not your fault. I could've said something, but you're always so on top of everything, and I'm . . ." I blow out a breath. "You said it last night. I'm a little over the top. I talk too much, and I laugh too loud, and I make jokes when I'm nervous. But that's also why I'm good at my job. Clients remember me. I make them laugh, and we build honest-to-goodness relationships. Mostly the women, I think I tend to piss of the execs."

He huffs a laugh.

"Anyway, last night, it didn't feel like you had my back. It felt like you wanted me to do things like you do, but I don't think that's how a company or a relationship thrives." I almost stop right there because I have little to no experience running either a company or a relationship, but it feels so right, I soldier on. "We have to champion what makes each of us tick. Even when there's a flip side. Megan's rose-colored glasses make gorgeous, hopeful designs. Sam's realism saves us money every day. I'd like to think my personality attracts and keeps the types of clients we want here, and I'm not saying I don't have things to change—"

"No. I get it." Garrett stops me, and the room stills around us. "I didn't mean to make you feel—" He draws a breath and meets my eyes. "I was nervous. I thought I was protecting the account."

"I know."

He taps the pen box against his palm. "Okay. So . . . we're good?"

I nod. "Yeah. We're good."

He turns again to the door, then hesitates, "I might not have paid attention when I should've, but for what it's worth, I asked you last night because I think you're fun. I did enjoy spending time with you."

I smile. "Thanks. That's nice."

He nods once, then walks back to his office.

eighteen

SAM CACKLES, picking up her fork and stabbing it into her Cobb salad. "He thought Calder was into me?"

"I know! I mean, not that he couldn't be, but where did he get that idea?"

She shrugs and swallows before saying, "You know what this means. You have to listen to me forever now."

I shake my head. "I barely know him."

She grins. "You know you like kissing him. And that he buys you fancy glasses."

"So much better than a pen, right?" I look behind me to make sure Garrett isn't standing in the hall. His door's closed. I breathe a sigh of relief. "I'm proud of myself. I told Garrett the truth."

"You did. You were a very big girl today."

I beam at her. I might not have received that kind of praise from my own parents, but she's an excellent surrogate. "I'd marry you, I think."

"Yeah?" Sam crunches on a forkful of lettuce. "I'm messy."

"Perfect. Then I'd feel like the clean one for once."

"We could run together in the morning."

I screw up my face. "Forgot about that. Deal breaker."

Sam laughs. "It's too bad we didn't have this discussion earlier. I would've opted out of our singles' night at Smash Point."

My eyes fly wide. "Is that tonight?"

"Mmhmm. Did you bring your stuff?"

"Definitely."

Sam reaches for her water bottle. "We'll stop by your apartment on the way."

* * *

ALECIA

> Sam and I are heading to Smash Point for the singles thing. Are you there?

CALDER

> You're single?

> I don't think anyone's locked all of this down yet

> Huh. Someone told me you were making out with a guy in the parking lot. Weird

> Yeah, not sure where you're getting your information

> I'll be there

. . .

Sam tries to grab my phone, but I throw myself at the window. "Stop! You're going to kill us all!"

She laughs, only swerving a little as she puts her hand back on the wheel. "You're smiling like a lunatic."

"That's normal."

"What did he text you?"

I hold my phone like it's piece of delicate fruit. "I'll show you when we park. It's not as good if I say it out loud!"

Sam rolls her eyes and turns up the music. The sky does that neon sherbet thing that makes you forget there's anything wrong happening in the world, and we sing-shout along to Rascal Flatts the rest of the drive. When we finally park, I keep my promise and let Sam read through my texts with Calder. We're both a little giddy as we walk into the club.

Luckily, Smash Point is buzzing when we enter. We're barely on time, so Sam pulls out her wallet to check in, but Space Buns waves her off. "You're covered."

My eyes narrow. "Does she have a membership?"

Sam frowns. "I didn't—"

"She does. Paid monthly."

I yank on Sam's arm before she can say anything. "I think Calder got us free memberships," I hiss as we race to the back where our group is gathered.

"What? Because of our lessons?"

I nod. "Yeah, when I came with Garrett, they said I had one, too."

"Well, that's amaz—" She stops, holding on the "z," her eyes fixed dead ahead.

A man stands on a flipped-over crate, calling everyone to attention. He's tall and tan with dark puppy-dog eyes.

Sam scoffs. "What is it with these guys? It's like they're factory made."

I give her the side eye.

"Not Calder. I'm just saying."

"You know, one of these days you could actually give one of 'these guys' the time of day. You might find out they're not all bad."

We barely make it to the tables by the time Justin—I find his name on the tag pinned to the front of his shirt—starts explaining the rules for the night.

"Each of you filled out a questionnaire online, yes?"

The group nods in unison, but I don't.

I lean over to Sam. "There was a questionnaire?"

"Didn't you see it in the app?"

No, I did not see it in the app.

Justin continues, "We've got them printed up and posted there." He points to the wall between our courts. "So if you find someone you want to know more about, you can read their answers and get some talking points. Or, you know, just ask them." That gets some chuckles. "Warm-ups are three minutes, then a game to five. Green wristbands rotate."

I look down and see that most people already have on either a green or blue wristband. Failed twice already, excellent.

"Where's your questionnaire?" A voice sounds behind me, and I jump. I'm already smiling before I see Calder's face.

"Must've forgotten. Where's yours?"

He shrugs. "Still filling it out."

My eyebrows shoot up. "Oh yeah?"

The whistle blows, and we scatter. My first partner is a guy in 80s-patterned shorts, which are legitimately cool. My second is a software engineer who . . . fits the stereotype of a software engineer, and my third is a dentist who seems nice enough that I motion to Sam to get him on her list.

"Ladies, looking good out here!" a voice calls, and I turn to see Frank along the fence, his right leg in a boot.

"Hey!" I jog over. "How are you feeling?"

"Oh, it's coming along. Another couple of weeks and I'll be ready to try it out."

Sam comes over from her court to say hi. We may have only had one lesson with Frank, but he certainly made an impression.

"Looks like Calder got you whipped into shape while I was gone."

I nod. "He's a task master."

Sam somehow keeps a straight face as she says, "So much drilling."

Frank chuckles. "Well, glad to hear it. Looks like I better let you go."

Sam's partner waves her over, and when I turn back to my court, my heart lights up. "Speak of the devil."

My fourth partner is Calder.

He saunters onto the court with a lackadaisical, "Hey."

I stifle a smile. I don't know how I ever thought he was in a bad mood all the time. Now his expression looks less broody, more thoughtful. "Having a good time?"

"The best. You?"

"Oh, definitely."

Calder tosses the ball over the net, and we get into a dinking rhythm. "So what do we do now?"

"I think you're supposed to be charming or something."

"Oh. Perfect. My specialty."

I snort.

"Seems it's already working."

I don't know what we talk about for the next five minutes because I don't think I'm physically inhabiting my body. I'm floating. Living in the rafters.

By the time we play our mini game, I'm barely capable of holding up my paddle.

"What are you doing?" Calder frowns at me when I miss a block at the net.

I smile back. "I don't know."

His lips twitch. "You're not paying attention."

"Yeah. It's hard. I'm a bit distracted."

He blows out a breath. "If you tell me there's another spider—"

I bark a laugh. "No, no spider."

"Then get your head in the game, Mabel."

A comment like that isn't helping, but I do my best. We end up squeaking out a win 5-4 and after we tap paddles, Calder turns to me. "That was a terrible showing."

A laugh bubbles up my throat. "I know. I'm sorry."

"Your instructor must be pretty bad."

"No, this is my fault. He's great."

Smile lines form at the corners of his eyes. "I probably shouldn't look at your questionnaire then."

I give an "oh, shucks" swing of my arm. "I didn't finish it, so you couldn't even if you wanted to. Probably a defense mechanism."

Calder grunts. "Well, luckily your instructor saw that coming. So he took care of it." He turns and walks to his bag, pulling out an old-school manila folder.

"What is—?"

He hands it to me. "You can post them if you want."

I stare at the folder, then flip it open to see a form with Calder's name written at the top. And behind it—

"You filled one out for me?"

He scrubs a hand over his jaw. "I think you'll find it's extremely accurate."

nineteen

I FIND a quiet table away from the group and pull out the first sheet. There are enough people here, they won't miss me for a round.

"Pierce, Frederick Calder" is scrawled across the top of a lined piece of paper. Very official. I look up with a grin, but Calder isn't watching. He isn't . . . on the court anymore either. Strange.

I keep reading.

1. What's your ideal Saturday?
Sleeping in. Then pickleball two ways.

I choke on my laugh and search for him again. *Where the hell is he?*

2. Biggest turn-on?

You already know this.

Uh, yes. Pickleball skorts.

3. Biggest red flag?

You already know this.

True again. People who swear they can only play with one brand of balls.

4. What's your type?

Women who risk their lives to rescue animals that will die next week.

I slap a hand over my mouth to keep from squealing. My heart feels like it's been dunked in carbonated water, all bubbly and popping.

I rip out the second sheet with my name on the top, and my breathing hitches. There aren't four questions listed like his. I scan the page, then flip it over. There are twenty-eight questions?

1. What's your favorite snack?

Those cinnamon almond butter biscuit things. You always have one in your bag.

2. What's your favorite color?

Blue.

I blink and look down. My skirt is sky blue, and my tank top is navy. Huh.

3. Where did you grow up?

Loveland, but you got your degree at CU Boulder.

I sit up straight. We've never talked about that. How does he—? I read through the other questions. *What's your favorite show? What's your makeup brand? What was your best date?*

The answers are all there.

"Hey! You disappeared for a minute. You good?" Sam jogs up and leans over the table. She barely glances at the paper in my hands. I'm immediately skeptical.

"You don't want to see what this is?"

Her eyes widen. "Oh! Sure, yeah. Please—"

"Sam."

She swallows hard. "Alecia."

My jaw drops. "You were in on this!"

Sam thinks about denying it, but can't do it. Her face lights up. "He had so many questions."

"When did you talk with him?"

"Most of last week."

"What!?"

"Yeah, he got my number from Garrett, and—"

"He texted Garrett about you?"

"Yeah, he—"

We both land at the same realization at the exact same time and burst out laughing. That's why Garrett thought Calder was into Sam.

"Why didn't you tell me?"

She throws out her hands and nearly sweeps her new paddle onto the floor. "Because he said he had this whole plan. And he was so serious about it. It was adorable."

"But he didn't know you and I were—" Oooh. Yes he did. He has access to the app and we were both signed up for singles' night. He knew we were coming before I even texted.

My mind spins. "So he had this planned before last night."

"Yeah, babe."

I shove the papers back into the folder. "Where is he?" She scans the courts just like I do, but we both come up empty. "Did he leave? I swear."

I run to my bag, shove the folder in, grab my phone, then bolt to the front doors, and push out to the parking lot. I search for his car, but when I don't see it right away, I dial his number.

"Hello?"

"What the hell? You give me that and then take off?"

He laughs. "I didn't take off."

"Well, you're not inside. Are you in the back or something? I came outside, but your car isn't here, so—"

"Alecia. Look up."

I stop and lift my eyes. Calder's there. Halfway down the first aisle of the lot. Half obscured by Pete and Julie's SUV.

I click off the phone and dart toward him.

twenty

I DON'T EVEN REMEMBER DECIDING to move, and then I can only hear my sneakers slapping the asphalt as I jog toward him. Calder meets me halfway, and for a second we just stand there, breathing hard.

"You were planning to give me that. Even before last night."

He nods. "Yeah."

"That could've been really creepy."

"Right. I thought about that."

"It wasn't, though."

He lets out a puff of air. "Well. I'm better when I write things down."

"I'd say you're pretty good in person." I can't wait another second. I loop my arms around his neck and kiss him.

His hands slide over the small of my back, crossing like good shapewear and holding me snug. I feel safe and protected in his arms, like I could burrow in deep and sleep for the winter. And what a hibernation it would be with that mouth. His lips are dragging over my jaw, sending a

165

jolt to my middle as he kisses my neck. I curl my fingers in his hair, in his T-shirt.

The wind picks up, and I tuck myself closer, nudging his lips back to mine. I warm my hands on his cheeks and kiss him deeply, my tongue brushing his.

When I start to shiver, he grasps my wrists. "Are we going back in there?" His voice is hoarse, and I'm instantly obsessed.

I groan. "My stuff is still there. I left my bag—"

Calder moves, leading me to his car. "Get in. I'll go grab it."

"Are you sure?"

"You're freezing."

"I know, but—"

"And I don't trust you to get it without stopping to talk to a hundred people."

I nod soberly. "That's fair."

He hands me the keys, and my eyes light up. "What if I steal your car?"

"Then I'll steal your wallet."

I scoff. "Rude!"

Calder closes the door and jogs into the building, the wind sending ripples of T-shirt across his back. I snoop, just a little, but he doesn't have anything damning in his consoles. Just gum, a phone charger, and—ooh. I pull out a small bag of dog treats. That was information.

I swear he was only gone for five seconds when he opens the back door and catches me red-handed. I jump, dropping the bag back in the console and closing it while he puts my bag on the seat.

"You have a dog?" I ask.

"No. It's for my sister's dog. I take him to the park on Sundays."

"It's the perfect way to have a pet."

"One day a week." Calder settles into the driver's seat and presses the start button, then grabs my hand and holds it. "So wher—"

"My place." I say too fast. My face reddens. "If you want. I didn't—"

"Are you sure? You have work in the morning."

"I could call in sick."

He gives me a look.

"I know, I know. Lies aren't a good start to a relationship. But if I don't get any sleep and I honestly feel sick—"

"Why wouldn't you get any sleep?"

I laugh.

He somehow keeps a straight face. "Are we going to watch movies? Play board games?"

My stomach flips. "Frederick Calder."

"You're blushing."

"Well, you make me blush."

He has a self-satisfied smirk when he puts the car in drive. We're barely out of the parking lot before I start in on the questions. I discover he grew up in a postage-stamp town in the Midwest, the kind where the biggest weekend event is the county fair tractor pull. His parents ran a hardware store, his older sister moved here with her husband shortly after he did and teaches middle school art in Arvada. He went to college in Indiana on a tennis scholarship, got a degree in kinesiology, and found pickleball by accident during his senior year when a teammate dragged him to a rec league tournament. He walked away with a medal and a mild obsession.

A few sponsors, a few trophies, and a well-timed Denver tournament later, he decided the mountains were home. These days he splits his time between coaching at Smash Point and working as a sports rehab specialist at a physical therapy clinic. The same one that treated his shoulder when he wrecked it.

As we turn down my street, my confidence starts to wobble. "Just a warning," I say, fidgeting with the zipper on the hoodie I grabbed from my bag. "My apartment is a work in progress."

"No risk, no reward."

I point, and he pulls up to the curb. "And the reward is movies?"

Calder puts the car in park. "Or board games. Either one."

I laugh and get out, pulling my bag from the back. Calder grabs his, and the logistics of the situation flood my head. It's a rare occurrence. "I didn't think about clothes for you. Should we have stopped at your place?"

He pats his bag. "I've got a clean set."

I raise an eyebrow. "Confident, huh?"

He chuckles. "I teach most days and then have to go to the office. I always have extra clothes."

"Uh-huh." I turn to the entrance.

"I'm serious."

"Yeah. I believe you."

Calder sneaks up behind me and slaps my hip, and I yelp. We walk through the lobby and take the stairs to the second floor. When I unlock the door, I see my place through his eyes for the first time. The living room is a collage of colors—leather couch with mismatched throw pillows, a bright yellow lamp, art prints that range from landscapes to abstracts. The slightly haggard decorative fig tree I got from my downstairs neighbor when he moved.

Calder steps inside slowly, taking his time to look around the room. "This fits."

I smile, a little self-conscious. "Too much color?"

"No. Exactly right."

My chest feels like an overfilled balloon. "Okay, well, if you want to shower, I can make us something to eat. Wait, you're not a vegan are you?" I definitely should've asked that question on the way over.

He gives me a quizzical look. "No, why?"

I blow out a relieved breath. "Good. That could've been really bad."

"Because?"

"Oh. Because I would never."

He laughs out loud. "That's your red flag?"

"Are you kidding? We could never have nachos late at night? Or DoorDash greasy tacos? Order Thai basil pork?"

Calder stills, adjusting the bag on his shoulder.

"What?"

He shakes his head. "Nothing. That all sounds good." He sniffs and clears his throat. "Shower is . . ."

"Oh right, just down the hall. Bedroom is on the right. I have another bathroom that way," I point to the room behind the table, "but mine's better."

He nods and heads toward my room.

"Towels are in the cabinet, top shelf." I try not to sound flustered, but I'm already imagining him in my shower. I briefly consider joining him, but I tried that once and it wasn't nearly as sexy as advertised. I was freezing, and there were no good angles.

When he disappears down the hallway, I press both hands to my face and exhale. Then I busy myself in the kitchen, pulling out pasta, tomatoes, basil. Something I can make on autopilot since my rational brain is completely offline.

Calder is in my house. He kissed me twice and now he's naked in my house.

The shower starts. I focus on chopping tomatoes, humming under my breath. The scent of garlic and olive oil fills the air by the time he reappears in joggers and a clean T-shirt, his hair damp and messy.

He watches me stir the pan, amused. "You cook."

"I do. Rarely. I'm trying to impress you."

"Mission accomplished." He leans against the counter.

"It just has to simmer for a sec. If I go rinse off, can you drain the pasta when the timer goes off?"

He nods. "Yeah, of course." *Green flags, A.* I dry my hands on the dish towel and round the counter, planting a kiss on his cheek before taking my bag to my room.

I've never taken a faster shower. Turns out I did have time to wash my hair last night, because I accomplish it now in less than three minutes. I rush to towel off and wrap my hair so it can dry for a few seconds while I moisturize. I comb it out and put on my nicest sweats and a tank top, then hit the light and leave the lamp on next to the bed.

I step into the living room barefoot and stop short. Calder's sitting at my table, one arm draped casually over the back of the chair. The food is plated, and he's filled water cups with slices of lemon.

"I found them in the fridge. Hope that's okay."

I smile. "Definitely." I walk over and sit next to him. "Hi."

"Hi." He leans over and kisses me.

I smile against his lips. "You smell like my soap."

He kisses me again, twisting my damp hair around his fingers, then pulls back and looks at me. I'm lost in those glacier pools when he says, "The food will get cold." He doesn't have to say the rest. I'm thinking the same thing.

"I have a microwave."

He pulls me up off the chair so fast, I gasp. "Calder!" His laugh is rough as he moves me back and scoops me into his arms. I curl into him since the hall is narrow, and he has to adjust our angle twice to make it through the bedroom door.

Lamp light for the win. He drops me onto my floral comforter and lowers himself over me. *Yes. This.* I reach for him, threading my legs with his. "I love board games."

"Mm. My favorite."

I tug his shirt up, feeling goosebumps rise on his skin under my fingers. I touch even lighter, and grin when he shivers.

"Proud of yourself?"

"Very."

He pushes himself up and rolls me onto my stomach, then bunches up my tank top, sucking in a breath when he sees that's all I was wearing. Calder brushes his knuckles along my spine, then rubs my shoulders, pressing his thumbs into every tense muscle.

"That. Is the most amazing thing in the world," I murmur into my pillow. The next thing I feel is the scruff of his jaw against my skin. His hands clasped over my hips.

Okay. I stand corrected.

I reach back and wrap my hands over whatever I can find. His wrists, his forearms, and when I can't take it a second longer, I flip back to face him and pull his shirt up. He straightens and takes it off, tossing it on the floor.

I suck in a breath, taking him in. The dark hair on his chest, the lines of muscle that expand and shift with his inhale.

He settles next to me, his fingers splaying over my stomach as he finds my mouth. He listens to my breath, notices when my body reacts to a kiss or a touch, and does it again to make sure he got it right. All that intensity and focus he uses on the court is doubly effective in this situation, and I can't believe I ever thought I could only want this for a night.

My touch grows more desperate. "I love melatonin."

Calder laughs. "What?"

"Shh. It's our inside joke."

It takes him a second, but when he remembers, he kisses me harder. I push at the waistband of his joggers, done with subtlety.

He cups my face in his hand and tilts my head, kissing a line down my throat. "Enchanted. Definitely enchanted."

twenty-one

SAM ALREADY HAS a lemon-ginger tea steaming on her desk when I walk in. I close the door behind me and lean against it, trying for casual and failing spectacularly.

She grins. "You didn't call in sick."

I scoff. "I'd never do that." I tried three times, but Calder wouldn't let me. He was doing dishes in his boxer briefs when I left. I wasn't mad about it.

"Well?" Her eyes glitter as she leans back in her chair and twists back and forth.

We both know stalling isn't my strong suit. I launch myself into the egg chair and start in with every detail from the time we left Smash Point.

Sam's cup is empty by the time I finish. It didn't take Calder nearly that long.

Sam throws a pen cap at me. "Ugh. I'm so jealous."

I laugh and toss it back on the desk. "How was the rest of singles' night?"

She sighs. "Fun until I heard all that."

"Did you see Justin again?"

Sam leans forward, lowering her voice even though the

door is closed. "He's the owner's son. Talk about nepotism. I guess he works with some big-name pickleball company. Travels around and does tournaments or something."

I purse my lips. "Well, that sucks."

"Does it?"

I raise an eyebrow. "We could find out when he's in town—"

"No! Do not ask Calder. I have less than zero interest."

"But nights like last night only happen when—"

"No."

I mime my lips being zipped. But we both know that's happening. If she's dishing out matchmaker, she better be able to take it.

Sam catches something through the glass of her office door. Her eyes widen, and she motions for me to come to her side of the desk. "Look natural. Pretend I'm—" She reaches for a folder of samples and flips it open. "There. I'm showing you something you need to really consider and take your time with."

I pretend to pore over the swatches from the wedding invitations we did for the daughter of a real estate mogul last month, while sneaking a glance through the glass at the breakroom.

Garrett and Megan are posted at the counter, laughing over something on Megan's phone. He's leaning into her, and she tilts her head toward him, her arm brushing his when she swipes on the screen.

"Maybe you changed him after all."

I sigh. "Just prepping him for the goddess."

"You're so selfless." Sam pushes a book to the side and grabs the notepad I gave her, picking up her pen. She scratches out "Presses bridge of nose" and writes "Laughs with teeth."

I cough a laugh and take the pen from her, crossing out "Hand touches face" and replacing it with "Looks down shirt."

Sam devolves into giggles. We watch as Megan nudges his arm, and Garrett rinses her mug.

"We should invite Megan to play at Smash Point sometime," I say.

Sam smiles. "I was thinking the exact same thing."

My phone buzzes in my pocket, and I pull it out. It's from Calder. A screenshot of tonight's schedule with the round robin circled at 7 p.m.

You two in?

Sam plucks it from my hand.

Yes. As long as Natasha and Ben are going to be there. I demand vengeance. -Sam

Vengeance is usually saved for DUPR events. I'll see what I can do

"I need one of those." Sam hands my phone back.

"What? A hot boyfriend?"

She snorts. "No, a DUPR."

I blow her a kiss before exiting to the hall, then open the chat with Calder.

. . .

ALECIA

> I have a confession to make

CALDER

> I already know you don't rinse your dishes. I emptied your dishwasher filter

I laugh, leaning against the wall so I don't barrel into someone coming around the corner.

> No, I think I'm one of those people

> Mabel, no

> I'm sorry. It just happened. I played with them, and I can't go back

> Frederick is my favorite brand of balls

* * *

See Sam and Justin's story in The Setup, Book #2 in Smash Point Social Club

Justin needs a plus-one for the pickleball tour his ex—and her celebrity boyfriend—are running.
Sam needs a distraction (and possibly a noncommittal make-out or two) that doesn't involve real feelings.

The deal is simple: fake date, make her jealous, win the breakup.
But between tournament stops, late-night drills, and a room with only one bed, the line between pretend and "play on" starts to blur...

Watch for Book #2 in Smash Point Social Club, *The Setup,* to see how long they can ignore the tension . . .

Tropes:
- Fake Dating
- Sizzling banter
- Only one bed
- Black cat/Retriever

Cindy Gunderson is a voice actress and award-winning author. Since she has commitment issues, she writes both sci-fi and fantasy, as well as contemporary romance and women's fiction under the pen name, Cynthia Gunderson.

When she is not typing away in a quiet corner of her local library, you can find her traveling with her family, narrating audiobooks, or happily digging in her garden. She loves acting and performing, beating her kids in card games, and playing ultimate frisbee with her handsome husband, Scott.

Cindy grew up in Alberta, Canada, but has lived most of her adult life between California and Colorado. She currently resides in the Denver metro area. Cindy holds a B.S. in Psychology from Brigham Young University.

Cindy's first novel Tier 1 was awarded First Place in Science Fiction at the 2021 CIPPA EVVY Awards and her women's fiction novel Yes, And was honored with the Indie Author Award's first place prize for the state of Colorado, 2023.